Cemetery Drive

Lucian Clark

This is a work of fiction. The characters and events portrayed in this book are fictitious. All names, places, characters and incidents are either the product of the author's imagination or are used fictitiously. Any similarity to real persons, living or dead, is coincidental and not intended by the author.

ISBN-13 (Print): 978-0-578-77817-4

ISBN-13 (eBook): 978-0-578-77818-1

Cover design by: K.M. Claude

Published by: Lucian Clark

Printed in the United States of America

To everyone who supported me and told me to go for it.

To my wife who supports all my dreams no matter how wild (but still within reason).

“Real revenge is making something of yourself.”

- Gerard Way

I.

Despite being on a busy highway, Helena's never looked packed. Friday and Saturday, usually the busiest nights for the other bars, seemed to have the same amount of vehicles in the parking lot as on a Wednesday. I had driven by the place many times on my way to work, but never once decided to give it a shot, until that night. Only a few of the lights in the sign still worked which cast a flickering red glow across the parking lot. It wasn't the most welcoming place on the street. Even the front door was a solid matte black, not exactly inviting, but to me, it spoke of some hidden promise. That night there was something calling to me about the quiet nature Helena's seemed to promise. Somewhere to have a drink or several and maybe quell that idea that you're alone for a minute. I needed that. There was a hush that fell over you the moment you walked into that dim and foggy glow. Eerie, but comforting.

A darkness blanketed the whole inside and the décor was fairly plain and uninspired. Along the far wall were a few neon signs of various colors, with the pink one bearing the name of the bar being the most obnoxious. Compared to the other signs, it seems like this one was the only one that had been replaced or put up in the last few years. As one entered, the bar took up the entire left-hand wall, with the rest of the establishment being filled with various billiard and wooden tables. The opposite wall had four booths which made the inside look more like a dingy diner than a bar. Half the hanging lights, which were mismatched chandeliers, were missing bulbs or had various brightness and hue ranging from bright white to dingy yellow. The ragtag bunch of people inside were talking quietly in groups among themselves, with the bar stools being mostly empty except for a few people evenly space throughout. None of them were talking to each other, enjoying their drinks in total silence. I took a seat at a booth, not wanting to get a drink quite yet.

When I first saw him, he was sitting in the far dark corner of the bar, partially shadowed by that neon pink sign above his head. If it wasn't for the way the light bounced off his black hair, I doubt I would have noticed him. The darkness inside of Helena's seemed to completely engulf him. It didn't take much for me to notice everyone was ignoring that gentleman in the corner. Their gazes never went in his direction. Not even the bartender stayed to chat with him, despite being extremely chatty (and even touchy) with the other bar-goers. In a rather ghostly manner, he would float over to fill the patron's glass and then move on. There was an almost clockwork feeling to the movements; stiff and formal. The complete change of demeanor seemed more out of place than the one on the receiving end.

Subtly was not the strong suit of this person at the end of the bar. Every article of clothing was black, which explained why he melted so thoroughly into the shadows. The black blouse he wore dipped down to expose pale skin, clearly meant to be worn by someone with breasts to show off. While I could not see them due to hiding in the deep darkness under the bar, I could bet his legs were encased in something equally as black and equally meant for his waifish frame. His dramatic apparel intrigued me even further. The exact opposite of my sandy hair and large frame, and the extremely masculine clients that were currently in the bar. There were a lot of baseball caps, t-shirts, and torn jeans.

It was this complete avoidance that drew me closer towards him. What was so wrong with this slight man that no one wanted anything to do with him? There wasn't anything...*off* about him, from what I could tell. He looked like the type that usually would just bat their eyes and never have to pay their tab again. So why was he all alone? When I sat next to him, he didn't even turn those big Bambi eyes towards me; he continued to stare forward at the wall across the bar. Maybe to him, the entire bar was haunted.

He had been crying. There was no doubt about that. Dark eyes were lined with red, his make-up streaking down his cheeks to leave small dark puddles on the bar. Still wet. Under his eyes were dark circles, deeper than the running mascara, eyeliner, and eye shadow. I couldn't tell if it was from crying, or something else since his skin was so pale in the dull glow of the bar. Even his fingernails were painted black, though the paint was chipping around the tips due to a clear nail biting habit. Every drink he took from his glass was drawn out, like he was sucking his time through that straw. The longer he took, the longer time froze. His black hair was held in a sad attempt at a bun, looking more like a rats' nest on the top of his head. Loose strands framed his face, unintentionally pulling more attention to the parallel streams down his cheeks.

There was a pull to his sad beauty that made me sit next to him, flag the bartender over, and order a drink for each of us. From my experience you usually don't see very many people like him in dives like this. Or really ever anymore. Goth (or would he be more emo?) was an early 2000s relic for the most part. Plus, if he stayed I would at least have some company to fill the night and an interesting story to listen to. Win-win. The bartender didn't say anything about my request, but he raised one bushy eyebrow in confusion before filling my order. He didn't need to say anything, that look said everything: "Why?" Why not? I answered with my grin.

He left soon after I sat next to him. I wasn't sure if it was my presence or acknowledgment of him that pushed him away. Maybe it was just time for him to leave. Regardless of the reason, I couldn't help but take it personally. Rejection stings. Most of all, he left before the drink I had ordered for him was ready. It had to be another time then, another night. Sighing, my fingers ran through my hair as I cursed myself for not trying sooner. Would I see him again? There was no name to even fill the void in my head, just a mystery and a feeling.

The thought of never seeing that gothic pretty boy again brought a twinge of sadness. Someone so unique definitely had stories to tell, or was at least an interesting conversationalist, right? I took a long sip of the beer I had bought him and crinkled my nose at the taste. Just your typical watered down, mass produced supermarket beer. Maybe I was wrong in my observation about him being interesting. Then it hit me. Everyone was avoiding him – everyone but me. That means the bar is full of regulars, including him. My original idea of him being out of place had to be incorrect, which only fueled my burning need to see him again. His story, whatever it may be, gnawed at my guts. Infatuation lit like a match, and me the moth to its flame.

Every night I started going to Helena's, searching. Not having a name to do my snooping in private made it impossible to quell my curiosity. When I thought of him my heart leaped into my throat. I needed to know why. I couldn't get him out of my head. When I wasn't working or drinking, I was thinking of that person huddled in the corner, highlighted by the neon pink glow. Of those big, dark, eyes brimming with tears. Of his queer dress and demeanor.

It wasn't without effort that I didn't know his name. No one at the bar seemed to know who I was talking about, and if they did, they didn't want to talk about him. They curled their lips and wrinkled their noses when I described him, but still gave no answers. If there was one thing I could figure out, it was that every regular wanted nothing to do with him. Why, I could not for the life of me figure out. What was his story? This slight, gentle seeming person had an entire bar that would not speak of him, yet still tolerated his presence. Obviously nothing heinous enough to warrant a ban, but bad enough to be ex-communicated among the local community. A harsh punishment still. So why not leave and go somewhere else? Why let him in at all? The harder I tried to figure out why, the more questions I had. I felt like a teenager with a high school crush again, and not in all the good ways either.

It was something like two weeks before I saw him again. At that point I was on the verge on giving up. Maybe I was wrong all along and he really was a ghost. Maybe the faces and the weird looks were because I was seeing things. But, to hallucinate a whole person like that? It wasn't *that* dark in Helena's. There was also the fact that there are only so many overpriced drinks my wallet could take. Going to a bar every night was not usually my thing. Drinking at home was more my style. Helped it was the cheaper option, too. Maybe our paths weren't meant to cross. Fate is not something that can be forced. I wouldn't have blamed him for not showing back up considering how he was treated. I thought I had just read the room wrong, or missed some sort of event prior to showing up that night. Wouldn't be the first time I was completely off on a hunch.

With the ice melting in my empty glass, I was

about to call it quits when he floated through the door. Silent and unnoticed, he took his spot in the shadowed corner, ordered his drink without a word, and got ready to ride out the night. His bag was placed under his stool, looped around his leg. Fingers ran through his hair, which ruined the bun that was pulled painfully tight on top of his head. Those big, dark eyes sparkled in what light they caught, filled to the brim and threatening to burst with tears. Dark streams down his cheeks showed that they already had at some point. The make-up that was smudged across his eyes and mouth still had the hallmarks of being meticulously done. Honestly I would have missed him slipping in if it wasn't for the sharp smell of perfume that suddenly overtook the corner of the bar; an aroma that cut through the thick smell of smoke and beer.

The bartender raised his eyebrow at me again as I moved to sit next to my recent obsession. This time, he was asking "Again?" as if the embarrassment of my first attempt hadn't stung enough. The slight man sitting in the darkness didn't even acknowledge me when I gave a simple hey, his eyes staring at the shelves behind the bar; unfocused. His dark hair covered most of his face. That look was something I had seen before. Gone – knock all you want, but no one is there – kind of gone. On top of his head there was a pair of large, dark sunglasses as well. Strange for this time of night; the sun was long gone. Did he arrive already drunk?

"Hey, remember me?" I asked, speaking louder this time. Reaching out slowly, my fingers grazed his shoulder to try and catch his attention. Even when you're that gone you still notice when someone touches you. Usually. An innocent enough gesture I thought, but his reaction was anything but. In a flash of motion he recoiled and pressed himself to the wall. His eyes were wide, like a cornered animal. Against his shirt his chest heaved as air hissed between his lips, which I noticed were red this time, as opposed to black.

Highlighted under the neon sign, purple bloomed across pale skin, causing his already full lips to swell on the left side of his face. It danced up the side, the swelling just barely missing his eye. The darkness of the bar and his hair had hid the worst of the damage, even showing the stitches on his cheek. A fight, more than likely. But this person in front of me, who looked like a strong wind would topple him, in a fight? I simply couldn't believe it. Was he mugged then? Was this what caused everyone to ignore him? But this was too fresh to be from two weeks ago.

"Oh jeeze, I'm so sorry...I didn't..." The words

trailed off as the black-haired one relaxed, slumping back into his seat. He buried his face into his hands and let out a single, heavy sob. Way to go, I thought to myself.

"Leave me alone." The words were heavily accented and not one I could easily place. "I beg of you, please." Those Bambi eyes turned to me, his eyeliner running down his face again in thick, inky rivulets. "It's really not worth it." A slender hand rested gently on top of mine, reassuring me that he'd be alright if I were to simply obey his request. I could only focus on how soft and warm his hands were.

"Huh?" The word fumbled out of my mouth, as I looked up from the delicate hand to its owner. His eyebrows knitted tightly together, which caused him to wince, and he sighed through clenched teeth.

"I said leave me alone." Much sterner this time, bordering on annoyed. Without an accent as well. Did he think I didn't understand him the first time?

"Let me buy you a drink or at least give me your name." I begged. Corny, but I didn't want this encounter to slip away like the first one almost had. My heart ached at thinking it would be another two weeks before I saw him again. *If* I saw him again after this. I was drawn to him. Maybe a little obsessed with him, one could say. Something about this mysterious person who seemed so out of place had my heart alight. With a name, at least I'd have something to follow up on. Learn enough to have an idea and move on, but I had to know. Something to ease the unrest in my mind every time I thought of him.

"Jacques. Jacques Dupont..." His accent was French, or somewhere that spoke French with a name like that. French Canadian, maybe? "Most people call me Jack though..." He spoke without looking at me. His fingers twitched around his glass as his eyes returned to staring behind the bar. He wanted to go away, but I wouldn't let him.

"Judah. Judah Moretti." I matched Jack's introduction. "Though everyone just calls me...Well, they just call me Judah." I laughed, shrugging as Jack gently shook his head. In the corner of his mouth, the smallest smile set in. Got 'em.

"Religious family with a name like Judah?" Jack spoke softly, still not looking at me. That familiar dullness was beginning to set in. He wasn't really here, carrying the conversation on autopilot as a formality. However, the way he said my name...I felt it. Almost purred it, like he enjoyed the sound of it.

"Nah. They just liked the way it sounded, I

guess. I never really asked about it. Not sure where I stand on that subject either." I turned my gaze to behind the bar. As I took a sip of my whiskey, I caught Jack taking a glance at me, forcefully pulling himself out of whatever hole he had climbed into. It only lasted a moment, as he pulled back the moment he realized I had noticed. At least I knew I wasn't completely repulsive to him. The idea of a shared interest caused my heart to flutter.

"Relapsed Catholic, myself." A matter of fact statement. Jack sighed heavily as he set his jaw. Teeth clenched tight enough I could see his muscles flexing all the way to his sharp cheekbones. Preparing himself for something he didn't want to do. Or bracing himself against that statement.

"You should go." Jack whispered, words that seemed hard to say.

"Why?" My question caused his shoulders to tense. I don't think he was expecting push back on this. Maybe this was why everyone avoided him – he wanted it that way.

"Trust me, you should leave now." Hissing almost, his jaw was clenched so tightly. A shadow moved to block the light behind me, belonging to the bartender, no doubt.

"Until next time, Jack." I smiled, running my

thumb over his hand before gently patting it. Jack recoiled, pulling his hand to his chest like I had bitten it. That hurt. Was I misreading the signs, yet again? I rose heavily from my seat, stepping to the side as to not bump into the bartender on the wrong side of the bar. Did he really need to breathe down my neck? I was leaving and it was almost closing time anyway.

"If there is a next time." Jack mumbled. The bartender followed me out, making sure I went to my car. At least they were looking out for one of theirs? Did they even consider him one of theirs or was I just some weirdo still? It took me until I was sitting in my car to register what Jack had actually said. I looked back over my shoulder, almost expecting to see the bartender and Jack both watching me. No one. Way to go, Judah. Surely, I had made a fool of myself. I left Helena's feeling like my stomach was made of lead.

II.

Jack was a literal ghost online. No Facebook. No Twitter. Not even an Instagram. You would think someone who put that much care into their appearance would at least be on Instagram. The only thing I could find under the name Jacques or Jack Dupont was an article about a charity event for suicide awareness about six years ago. The kid in the photo did not look like Jack though. Closely cropped brown hair, no make-up, and a Catholic school uniform. But those big, brown eyes were unmistakable even without the tears and eyeliner. That was definitely Jack standing next to someone by the name of Gideon Bellview. Apparently Gideon was some big tech guy who donated something like a million dollars to the cause under Jack's name. As I tried to dig a bit more, I kept running into suggestions for Gideon Bellview. Almost every article that came up mentioned the man, so he had to be important, right? Why would he have decided to donate to Jack's cause? Despite my experience in the field of technology, I had no idea who Gideon Bellview was. The name didn't ring any bells, but then again I was in application development. Was he someone who knew Jack, or hell, an uncle or his father? Looked old enough to be in the photos anyway.

Turns out Gideon Bellview wasn't related to Jack, quite the opposite actually. At almost twice Jack's age, Gideon was his husband. Every photo of Mr. Bellview had Jack either at his side, or shrinking away from the camera with sunglasses on and his hand up. The articles barely even mentioned him by name, which was strange. Gideon always seemed to tower over Jack, not just due to Jack's slight frame, but also because of his demeanor. He almost seemed like he was guarding Jack. Dude was built like a linebacker. It would be surprising if Gideon didn't play football in high school. Kind of ironic for a tech mogul.

So, Jack was married. Interesting. I never noticed a ring on Jack's finger. There were no articles about a divorce, which meant he went to Helena's trying to hide his marriage. In fact, the most recent was from a week ago, talking about some charity event. In all the photos, Gideon was beaming, with an arm wrapped tightly around Jack. What was his deal? Once again, more questions than answers.

All the articles were about how successful Gideon was, having inherited the business from his father, or about the wedding and how shocked – and disappointed – everyone was with the news that Gideon was gay. The articles repeatedly talked about how they met through that mental health and suicide awareness charity. After his generous donation, Jack and Gideon moved quick. They married several months later, with Jack still not yet nineteen. Real scandalous shit. It seems like Jack became a house husband, barely mentioned as the articles went on. The oldest articles still excluded his full name referring to him as just Jack or Gideon's lover which explained why he was so hard to find. Gideon was almost as elusive as Jack, and probably would have been if it wasn't for the preexisting money and fame. As a college football player (called it), not much was said about him. Straight facts such as height (6'3") weight (270lbs), hometown (Newark, NJ) and the same information about his money, success, and marriage, over and over again. Another dead end.

I doubt Jack was looking for hook-ups since the entire bar avoided him like a rat with the plague. Even when I tried to approach him, he did his best to avoid me and push me away when I persisted. He wasn't there for the chit-chat either. So why did he go to Helena's? What was his game? Some type of retreat? Away from where? His marriage with an absolute tank of a husband, who had money to back up those hard and chiseled looks? Images of that purple and blue galaxy across his face came back to mind. A coincidence? Suddenly the body language in all those photos looked a lot more sinister.

Maybe I was imagining things and, while his marriage may not have been perfect, some nights Jack just needed to get away? Seemed pretty normal to me. What if he got into a fight that first night? Got mugged? Just because he has one bruise doesn't mean anything. I was imagining things and going there to be away after a lover's spat would explain the distance between visits too. My stomach rolled and clenched, spilling bile into my throat. Something didn't sit right with me about the whole thing. If that was the truth, why was he so damned afraid? But, abuse? Christ, Judah. The fuck is wrong with you? Time for a shot and to call it a night.

~~~~~~~~~~~~~~~~~~~~~~~~~~~~

The next night I went to Helena's as usual. Going had become a habit and no one bothered me, which was a bonus. After working with people all day sometimes you just want to exist outside of the world. Helena's offered that space for me. Might as well stop by, have a few drinks, and maybe catch a glimpse of my mystery man. I would occasionally
~~~~~~~~~~~~~~~~~~~~~~~~~~~~

still see Jack, but he always acted as if he was avoiding me. Every time he left, I felt that familiar pang in my stomach. He said to leave him alone though, so I did. Never ignoring him though, I would send the occasional drink down and wave at him. Had to let him know I was still interested in talking to him, even if he wasn't interested in talking to me. The drinks were never sent back or ignored, so I hoped there was still a shot. Pun intended.

I'm not quite sure what changed, but one night Jack sat next to me – not in the corner under the neon pink sign like he normally did. He sat right next to me in the middle of the bar and locked his eyes with mine. Tonight he wore a long black dress that fell to his ankles. A seemingly plain outfit if not for the fine mesh that covered his upper chest, shoulders, and arms. Once again, clearly meant for someone with cleavage.

"Why?" No hello, no good evening, nothing. I blinked in surprise, which seemed to annoy him. He sighed and rubbed his temples. "What is it? What do you want? Money?" Sleek fingers started to fumble in his bag, nails still painted black but accented with gold stars and silver moons that glittered in the light.

"Woah. What?" My hand eclipsed his as I stopped him, shaking my head. "No, I don't want money. Shit, this whole time you thought I wanted money?"

"Sex then? I'm married," he said. Married sounded weird on his tongue, like he wasn't used to telling people that. There was still no ring that I could see on his finger.

"Dude, I just think you seem interesting." Now it was Jack's turn to blink in surprise. Heat rose in my cheeks as we stared at each other. "Plus, you're beautiful." I blurted out.

Probably not the right thing to say as Jack ripped his hand from mine, curling a red stained lip. He went to say something, but I quickly cut him off. I couldn't ruin this chance. Not again. You don't get third chances, according to my knowledge. But then again, you aren't supposed to get second chances either, right?

"Sorry, sorry. Married." I raised my hands apologetically and he eyed me. There was a clarity to that look I hadn't seen before, maybe because this was the first time he wasn't crying. The tension was palpable, and the other patrons at the bar noticed it. One more misstep and Jack would be gone. All three of them got up and moved to one of the pool tables, leaving just Jack and I, staring at each other alone at the bar. Well, except for the bartender.

"I'm new-ish in town. I don't know anyone. Just humor me?" Jack settled down in his seat more as I spoke. He tapped the bar, thinking it over. He didn't say anything, but he didn't leave either. That's when I noticed the black cross that was behind his left ear. The lines were blurred and faded, a stick-and-poke from Lord knows how many years ago.

"Were you like twelve when you got that tattoo?" I asked, pointing. Sure, it wasn't the most polite way to ask about a tattoo, but the words came without a second thought.

Jack laughed and tucked his hair behind his ear, covering the offending tattoo.

"I was sixteen and rebellious! I was thinking about what would really piss my parents off. Something that they couldn't take or hide from the Catholic school." Jack laughed again and clicked his tongue. The bartender brought over Jack's usual, eyeing me with visible confusion.

"Whiskey." I ordered. Might as well if he was already over here. Jack looked at me and raised his beer.

"Guess we will be here a bit, huh?" He took a swig of beer. The flush on his cheeks was noticeable and his eyes swam with the dim lights of the bar.

"I figured a cross tattoo would really show

them." His fingers pressed against the black cross. A permanent mark of teenage rebellion with zero forethought. Ah, to be young and careless. He clicked his tongue again before shaking his head. "Well, now the good Lord has his mark on me whether I want Him to or not." Jack crossed himself before taking another drink. "Got away with it for a whole month too." I couldn't help but laugh which caused Jack to snort his beer and swat at me.

He was mesmerizing to watch. His hands accented everything he said, pointing and waving. Even the bartender was looking over and watching us as Jack told the story of his tattoos, all gotten in his youth, before he was married. There was a blackbird on his right shoulder signifying death, the snake around his right arm, complete with apple in its mouth to signify sin. At one point, he lifted his ankle-length black dress to show his entire left leg with an elaborate design of patterns, all radiating from a candle that took up his shin – hope. Every tattoo had a meaning.

"Hurt like a motherfucker." Jack said as he tapped the candle. "Worth it though. All reminders of the life I left behind." A familiar sadness crept into his voice and eyes as he spoke. Another drink to wash it down.

"For someone who considers themselves a

'lapsed Catholic' you certainly have a few religious symbols." I said, pointing specifically at the snake on his arm.

"Yea, well, religion is nothing but symbolism and I can appreciate good symbolism. Clearly." Jack smirked, raising an eyebrow like I amused him. Or he thought I was stupid.

"I have quite a few myself." I interjected.

"Religious symbols or tattoos?" Jack asked coyly.

"Tattoos-"

In a flash, Jack grabbed my right arm and flipped it, dragging his fingers along the knife I had tattooed there. His eyes sparkled as he watched his own fingers trace the lines, moving to the small birds I had along my elbow and upper arm. The decals on his fingernails glimmered in the light accenting his movements. My tattoos seemed to mesmerize him.

His fingers rested on my wrist, pressing into the set of lines I had there. "So, what do they mean?"

"Well, the ones under your fingers are cat whiskers, in memory of my childhood cat, Leo. The knife is literally because I thought it looked cool on the flash sheet. The birds were supposed to be a whole sunset piece but...I ran out of time and money." I shrugged. Jack looked disappointed. God, he was cute when he pouted.

"All things should have meaning." He said to me, matter of fact.

"If you want one with meaning, I have a bread and roses tattoo on my left side." I wiggled free of Jack's prying grasp to lift my shirt. I shuddered as Jack's fingers began to poke at the roses entwined with wheat grains across my ribs. "I'm a dirty socialist, sorry if that's a deal breaker." He ignored my politics as he continued to admire the tattoo across my side.

"I have roses on my hips. Black ones." Jack's words were flat. Too much focus on the details of the wheat. His finger even stopped on a spot where the red was beginning to fade on the roses indicating their age – my first tattoo and the one that hurt the most.

"I hope I can see them one day." No sooner had the words left my mouth did I stop. I bit my tongue. Did I really just say that? My heart thumped in my chest and I looked at Jack. His hands slowly pulled from my side and my stomach hurt. I was a fucking moron.

"I should leave." Jack stated plainly. All

friendliness from his voice was gone. Knocking back the rest of his third beer, and grabbing his bag in one swift motion, Jack was up from his seat. He kept his face downcast so I couldn't see his eyes, shadowed by his hair.

"I'm sorry, I didn't-" My pleas were ignored as Jack walked out the door. I had blown it. You don't get third chances. Not with a guy like that. My head thudded against the bar and I sighed heavily.

"Well, guess you're not gonna be kissing him, huh?" The bartender spoke, probably the first words he had spoken directly to me, as he dropped another whiskey in front of me.

"Yea, no shit, he's married." I grumbled and drained the glass.

Fuck.

III.

Night after night I would pay and leave, waiting for Jack to come back. I kept returning to Helena's, despite the fact you usually don't get third chances. Why not? Hope and determination had worked before. Eventually, everyone there started treating me like they treated Jack – a ghost. The bartender would just slide drinks down to me and that was that. The other regulars stopped gossiping when I came in. Nothing else really mattered at that time. I just needed to see him again. Time wasn't something I paid attention to unless it was time to leave and half the time I was practically dragged out by the bartender. All I needed was a chance to apologize for my behavior. Unfortunately, the next time I saw Jack, I quickly learned the true reason why everyone at Helena's turned a blind eye to his existence.

When I came in that unfortunate night, Jack was already there in his usual spot. However, a tall and muscular fellow was sitting next to him. The man was wearing a tailored suit and sunglasses perched on top of his cleanly shaven head. There was no mistaking that brutish yet handsome face that looked as if it were sculpted from brick. Gideon Bellview. He looked like every image I had seen on him online, despite some of them being over 10 years old. Either good genetics or the Botox money, my bet was on the latter. Giving them their own space, I sat a few seats away, ordered my drink, and kept an eye on them. Seeming to mock me, the light that normally sheltered Jack bounced off Gideon's head, obscuring Jack in almost total darkness. Gideon was much more intimidating in person.

Even with Gideon blocking my view I could still see Jack's outline. He was cowering against the wall. Whatever conversation they were having, I couldn't hear it over the music. Not a pleasant one from the way Jack was glued to the wall. Whatever was going on, no one paid them any mind. Everyone knew what was going on in that corner but they chose to ignore it. I caught Jack's eyes out of the corner of mine as Gideon shifted his weight in his seat. Fear flashed wildly in those dark sockets. He looked like a cornered mouse with a snake ready to strike, his eyes wide enough to be catching the light and filled with all-too-familiar tears.

I had to do something.

Tension filled the air as I walked straight up to Gideon. I could feel the eyes of everyone in the bar.

"Gideon Bellview, right? My name is Judah. I'm a friend of Jack's." I wiggled my fingers at Jack in a wave then extended my hand to Gideon which was met with confusion.

"Excuse me?" Gideon said in a monotone voice.

"I'm Judah. A friend of Jack's." I repeated the words, letting my hand fall to my side. Out of the corner of my eye, I watched Jack. He rolled his bottom lip through his teeth, chewing on it enough that I saw red. Was I making another mistake?

"Is that so, Jacques?" Goose bumps crept across my arms as Gideon drew out Jack's full name. Such contempt. Was this truly his husband?

"He's...he's spoken to me a few times." The words were barely audible. Jack hiccuped over a sob. "That's all." Why was Gideon so seemingly upset that I had spoken to Jack? It's not like anything was going on. Jack was already crying. What had they been fighting about before I came over? A shiver ran down my spine.

"Is this true," he paused, turning in his seat and towering over me, "Judah?" I'm not a small person, but sitting on the stool Gideon was still considerably bigger than me in both height and weight. The man was imposing, but I had squared up to men his size before. I had lost, but I stood my ground. That mattered more to me anyway.

"Yuh. I'm new in town. Figured Jack could help me out." I grinned and looked over at Jack who was staring at me with that same, distant watery gaze I had seen the first night at Helena's. He was gone, somewhere else. Somewhere far away from both Gideon and I.

Clearing my throat, I continued to trade pleasantries. "So, uh, Gideon, what brings you here tonight? Jack has mentioned you a few times, but I wondered why I never saw you." Gideon ignored my question, instead turning back to his husband.

"You know the rules." Gideon spoke coldly to Jack. Turning the corner of his lip upward into a sneer, Gideon grabbed Jack by the arm. Jack yelped and instantly clamped a hand over his mouth. Tears spilled down his cheeks as they turned towards Gideon.

"I-I'm sorry." Jack stammered as Gideon stood to his full height. He lifted Jack out of his seat and dragged him towards the door. Jack's apologies fell out his mouth a mile a minute, but I understood none of them. They were all directed at Gideon as he dragged him through the front door. The slamming door echoed through out the bar and I realized everyone was still staring at me. Every single one of them had their mouth open in disbelief.

"What?" A coldness shot through me as I looked at each one of those faces. My heart stopped. I understood why no one talked to Jack. It wasn't that they didn't want to, it's that they couldn't. Had Gideon threatened every one of them? Could he do that?

By the time I ran to the door, they were gone.

The words Gideon had spoken to Jack before they left rang through my head. "You know the rules". What were the rules? Was Jack not allowed to talk to anyone at Helena's? Why? Gideon had seemed truly pissed off that this had happened.

Meeting Gideon left a sour taste in my mouth. Everything was wrong. The way he talked to Jack. The way he looked at him. There was no love there, only anger and disdain – contempt. How could Jack stay with someone like that? Let alone for years? Alcohol mixed with bile in my mouth at the thought.

Maybe it wasn't always like that and I caught Gideon on a bad night? Maybe the "rules" were something else. But, even on a bad night, who controls who their partner talks to like that? Gideon seemed offended that I had even so much as addressed Jack, let alone in a friendly manner, several times. Would explain why everyone in Helena's avoided Jack if that is how Gideon treated people who talked to his husband. "Jealous type" didn't even begin to cover it.

~~~~~~~~~~~~~~~~~~~~~~~~~~~~~

It was a week before I saw Jack again. He slunk into the bar, hands clutched to his chest as he sat in his spot. His eyes were downcast and he seemed to be nervously fidgeting with something around his neck. The golden ring caught the light and I realized it was his wedding band. Had he always worn it like that? I didn't think so considering how low-cut some of his previous outfits had been.

I moved next to him like I always did. He glanced over at me and smiled faintly. Not the type of greeting I expected after the last meeting. We sat in quiet for awhile. The last time I had seen him, Gideon was sitting where I was. My stomach rolled at the thought of being that close to that man. I had no idea where to start or what to say or what to even do. Apologize, I thought to myself. That was the only thing I could think to do but before I swallowed my nerves, Jack spoke.
~~~~~~~~~~~~~~~~~~~~~~~~~~~~~

- III. -

"So...that was my husband. Gideon Bellview." His words were flat. Eerily monotone like Gideon. They were said out of the necessity to say something. Anything. At this point I think Jack was looking for a way to just talk to someone who wasn't Gideon. Or were they out of defiance? Gideon *had* been angry we were speaking to each other.

"How...how did you and Gideon meet?" Trying to make some form of small talk to fill the silence even though I knew the answer. I hid my awkwardness by sipping my drink and refusing to put it down. Jack's face fell and I felt my stomach drop again. Probably shouldn't be asking those kinds of questions, all things considered. Maybe I misread what Jack was doing. Was he trying to tell me to back off? My stomach started to flip now. Jack broke the awkward silence. Again.

"Some charity event. Gideon says he fell in love with me the moment he saw me." Jack snorted and set his jaw as he spoke. "I was nineteen when we got married. Barely out of high school. I dropped out of college on his suggestion." Jack drained his drink with a grimace.

"I, umm..." How do you admit to someone that you've been practically stalking them? Well, there was no going back now. At this point I had lost count of my chances, so what would another be? "I saw the articles. Back when we first met, I was trying to find you on Facebook and couldn't find anything so I put your name into Google and..." I trailed off as I realized I was going nowhere.

"Gideon doesn't want me to have one." He said the words so nonchalantly. "I kind of agree. Nothing but drama anyway and I know my family would use it somehow to get at me." He waved at the bartender before taking a sip of the drink that was brought. "They uh...didn't agree with me marrying Gideon. Catholic and all." He dryly chuckled.

"I'm sorry." I placed my hand lightly on his arm. He flinched away from the touch.

"Don't..." Jack whispered, but I understood and removed my hand. There was no need to give Gideon another excuse than we already were.

"It's...I was never close with them anyway." He continued. "They are very religious." His tongue clicked against his teeth as if he remembered he told me that already. "To the point where...well, let's just say there is a very specific Catholic demon who is said to turn men into homosexuals..." He chewed on his lip before placing his hand on my leg. "They don't even use my name anymore." The words came out on a bubble and he turned his face towards the sign, trying to hide his tears from me. Make-up streaked down his face and as a heavy sighing sob racked his body.

Next thing I knew, Jack pressed his face into my neck. He felt so small against me. His sobs were nearly silent, contained to soft hiccuping and jagged breaths. The sounds of someone who was used to hiding their tears. I could feel his fingers digging into my thighs, bunching the fabric of my jeans in his fists. When the fabric would slide free, his hands would desperately claw for it again.

All I could think about was how warm he was. His body felt like it was on fire with a feverish quality. I had this person, who I had only talked to a few times before, having a breakdown in my lap. And after a confrontation with his husband for having the audacity to speak to him nonetheless! Anger rose from the pit of my stomach. I wrapped my arms around him and pulled him close, not caring that, once again, all eyes were on us for this trespass. Judging us.

When Jack slowly peeled himself off of me, I ached. Suddenly I could feel the humid heat of the bar replacing where Jack once was. A slender finger gestured towards the door before placing a hand on my arm and rising from his seat. I followed after him, watching as he placed a cigarette between his black lips before he had even hit the door.

“I didn’t know you smoked.” I said, gladly

taking one of the cigarettes offered to me. It had been a long time since I had one and I welcomed the excuse. Smoke burned in just the right way.

"I don't have full out cry sessions on relative strangers in gay bars either, but here we are." Jack stated quite bitterly. I placed a hand on his shoulder and gently squeezed. A soft sigh escaped his lips along with the smoke as he leaned against my hand. "That was rude. My apologies." I never wanted to hear Jack apologize for anything again. It made me hurt.

"It's all good. You know what they say about assuming." I joked. Jack snorted looking like a cartoon bull as the smoke billowed from his nose. I sank into the bench outside the bar, amazed that it was still unoccupied. The closer it got to 3am, the more likely someone was passed-out drunk waiting on their ride. Even for a regulars-only bar, Helena's still had her fair share of late-night alcoholics. Myself included. Jack sat next to me with his elbows resting on his thighs. The cigarette hung from his mouth, just burning. His eyes were staring across the street, past the alleys and the businesses. A familiar look at this point. Disassociation. Where did he go to get away from the world?

"Gideon was the first person to tell me it was ok. That I wasn't a freak. That there wasn't something wrong with me. I fell for him so hard. So fast. I was a dumb teenager, of course I fell for him." Jack groped around next to him, grabbing my hand. He squeezed my fingers hard enough to hurt and kept going. "He let me be who I wanted to be. He let me explore make-up and clothing and fashion and music and..." His words trailed off. He pursed his lips together before taking a long drag of the cigarette.

"Gideon let me be me. He let me figure that out. He gave me a safe place. He left me live my life...and I loved him. I had freedom to be who I always wanted to be. I didn't have to act out for that taste. He supported me. In the beginning, he *loved* me." Tears spilled down Jack's cheeks yet again. He continued to squeeze my hand, refusing to let go.

"I'm sorry." I had no idea what to say in this situation. Jack laughed nervously, letting go to run his hand through his hair. This knocked his bun down, that hopeless black hair spilling around his face. He was gorgeous. Absolutely gorgeous. I moved closer, causing Jack to look over. Then I kissed him. There was no thought in my actions. Nothing more than instinct. I wanted to let him know that it was ok, that he shouldn't be sorry. And my dumb ass kissed him.

Before I realized I was even kissing him, Jack

was standing and leaving. His words were rapid and high pitched. The same way they had been that night I met Gideon. That same fear and anxiety. I could barely understand what was being said.

"-late. I should go. See you around, Judah. Thank you for listening. I can't be late. Gideon will be mad if I'm late." Jack wasn't leaving though. He was pacing back and forth in his place. His hands were wildly describing every word he spoke, running through his hair at what I assumed was the end of every statement. The bun that once held his hair was long gone and I could see his hair fell to just past his shoulders. His fingers grabbed fistfuls of those black locks, threatening to pull it out, and then letting it go. He got about ten feet away before stopping.

"Thank you for listening." Jack's words hit like a knife. The sadness held in his statement broke me.

"Jack, wait!" I called out, getting up and running after him. Long and quick strides to grab his arm and pull him back to me. Jack screamed before clamping his hands over his mouth and looking around. The red in his cheeks only accented his watery brown eyes. "Give me your phone." An old flip phone straight from the mid 2000s was placed into my hand without a word. I quickly put my number in, called my phone, and hung up. No name. No trace for Gideon to know it was me.

"That's my number. If you ever need me to listen. Please..." I wanted so bad to kiss him again. On my lips still remained the chalky taste of his lipstick. I could feel myself vibrating with the need, but this time I contained myself. Not that I wanted to, but I did. Jack left that night without another word.

IV.

The previous night had been on repeat in my head all day. All I could think of was what I should of said. What I shouldn't have done. How could I have been so stupid? Nothing I did yesterday seemed like the right thing to do, but it definitely felt right. Besides that the day passed without incident. As much as I had hoped, Jack did not call me. However, as I was getting ready for bed, that changed.

"Hello? This is-" I wasn't able to finish my greeting before Jack was spewing words from the other end of the line. He had been crying and may have been drunk. There was a strange quality to his voice that couldn't just be explained by crying. Was he calling me from Helena's? "Woah, woah. Slow down. I can't understand you."

"Come to Helena's. Now. Judah. *PLEASE!*" Jack's words were slurred and mumbled despite their desperation and panic. In fact, I had never heard him more drunk than he was right now. His voice said everything I needed to know.

"Give me fifteen." I was already pulling my shoes on before putting on my pants. Shit. "Maybe make it twenty."

"Make it ten." Jack hung up.

I got to Helena's in tweleve minutes. Jack was sitting on the bench outside, squeezing his phone until his knuckles were white. He kept looking around like he was a nervous teen about to do his first drug deal. When Jack noticed my car, he sprinted over. How did he know it was-

"I need to get away. Please. Take me anywhere. I just can't be *HERE* anymore." There was no time for me to answer before he was in my passenger seat, staring at me.

"Uh well..." It was past midnight. What would still be open at this hour? I guess Jack noticed my eyes looking at the donut shop across the street because he huffed and shook his head.

"Your place?" Jack had set his jaw and had this determined look in his eyes. This was already planned. Asking was merely a formality.

"You, uh...sure about that?" This was moving too quickly and what would Gideon think about going to my place this late at night?

"Gideon left me here. He took the car. He

thinks I'm stuck. We have until 3am." Jack spoke in staccatos. It was like if he didn't get the words out, he would never be able to leave. The dashboard glowed 12:23am. The time to get to my place and back left us with just about two hours in between.

"You sure?" I wanted nothing more than to have Jack to myself, away from the prying eyes at the bar. They wouldn't snitch to Gideon, but they wouldn't cover our asses either. "This is... dangerous."

"DRIVE!" Jack yelled as he slammed his hand against the glove box with tears streamed down his face. His reaction startled me. What had happened before I had gotten there that night? Everything was so wrong and weird, but I didn't question it. I didn't dare.

So, as commanded, I drove back to my place.

Approximately two hours. 120 minutes. No later either since, what if he came early to get Jack? Danger was thick in the air. Oppressive enough that we didn't talk for the drive back to my place, our brains running wild with what-ifs. At least, mine was. We knew the consequences. What the fuck was I doing? Jack was drunk and not thinking straight. Gideon would find out, of course he would. We were being stupid. We shouldn't be doing this. I should just tell Jack to go back to the bar and we'll figure something else out for another time. There had to be some other way, right?

Climbing the stairs to my apartment felt like it took up a large chunk of our limited time. Every step stretched on and on like a stairway to Heaven, or Hell if Gideon found out. Gideon wouldn't find out. He *couldn't* find out. Plus, what did we have to worry about? Jack was just over to talk and maybe have a drink or two. The door squealed loudly open as if to tell the world our secret. A deep sigh escaped from Jack as he entered my living room. Jack. In my apartment.

"Do you want a drink?" I offered as I took his jacket, if you could call the skimpy leather thing a jacket. It was cut to just above his ribs but was remarkably plain for Jack. Looking around my apartment, I definitely wasn't prepared for visitors. A pair of socks there, an empty take out bag over there, a few empty beer cans, and the sink full of dishes. It wasn't filthy, but it certainly wasn't how I would like with company over.

"No." Jack grabbed my hand which caused me to drop his coat. He kissed me. Jack kissed me!

I cupped Jack's face in my hands, kissing him as desperately as I felt. Jack's squeak of surprise and step backwards gave me pause for a moment. The concern dissipated the moment Jack stepped back into me. He began kissing me again. Our tongues pressed hard against each other's furiously trying to explore every inch. Jack's mouth tasted of beer and his lipstick, but sweeter in a way. His teeth grazed my lower lip and I shuddered which seemed to only spur Jack on harder as our teeth collided with the force of his kissing. My fingers danced along his spine feeling how thin the plain black long-sleeved shirt he wore was. Heat radiated through the fabric, only getting hotter under my fingers, as sweat started to cause it to cling to Jack's dampening skin.

Jack had me pinned against my own door with his teeth grazing along my jawbone and my neck. His hands shoved under my shirt and I shivered at their coldness. It didn't slow him down as he pulled my shirt over my head, moving to bite at my collarbone. Moaning softly only encouraged him more as his slender fingers traced designs along my stomach, then along my hips. His fingers danced along my sides, following the roses and wheat tattooed there. I had to bite my lip to contain a whine as my skin twitching under his touch.

"Jack..." I sighed his name. I was going to complain about the tickling but he turned those eyes up to me. In the pale light of my entrance way, those big, brown eyes sparkled. His bun had fallen loose and his face was framed with his black hair. Under the light I could see his brown roots starting to poke through. Why did he even try to keep his hair up? It was so gorgeous down. His pout was gone. There was a determination in that gaze I hadn't seen before. Determination mixed with something else – want. My heart hitched and I bit my lip harder, rolling it between my teeth. Fuck, I wanted Jack as badly as he wanted me. The door groaned as I leaned back against it. "Fuck...You sure about this?"

My hesitation seemed to only spur Jack on. He nestled his head into my neck, whining softly as his hands worked on my pants. His breath was so hot against my skin. Erratic. Another whine left his lips as he continued to fight with the button and at that moment I noticed he was shaking. His whole body was trembling against mine and he was pressing it hard against me. Gently, I grabbed his hands and pulled them to my lips. I kissed each trembling finger before holding them to my chest.

"We don't have to..." My words trailed off as Jack stepped away, fingers wrapping around my hands. "I'm perfectly happy to just be alone with you..." Jack shook his head. His hands pulled from mine and he ran his hand through his hair, looking off into the distance. A deep breath rattled through him and he turned back to me. Lithe fingers fully undid his bun before rolling the hair tie up my hand

and around my wrist.

"Please..." Jack whispered. His head tilted to the side as if it was supposed to be a question. He stepped back towards me and placed a hand on my bare chest. Dark eyes searched my face before he dropped to his knees. He was no longer shaking. Quick work was made of my fly, yanking my pants down my hips with a strength that surprised me. Jack focused on his work and pulled my underwear down to my thighs as well.

"You're already hard." Jack laughed the words, amused by my erection which danced only inches from his lips. I groaned while digging my fingers into his hair.

"Yeah well..." I had no justification. Why would I? His fingers ran along my shaft before gently pressing at the black star that rested just below my belly button.

"You never-" Jack didn't finish the words as he broke out in full out laughter as my face turned red. "Judah!"

"Young and drunk." I whimpered in embarrassment as I chewed on my lip. Was I really being mocked for my drunken teenage decisions now?

"And apparently a bit of a tramp." Jack

grinned knowingly, fingers tracing their way back to the tip of my cock with his thumb teasing the tip. My knees buckled slightly and I moaned. I couldn't even remember the last time I was this hot under someone's hands. And Jack was damn good with his hands. He continued to tease me, running his fingers up and down. When he finally grabbed my hips and took me into his mouth, I almost came then and there.

His tongue mimicked the playful nature of his fingers. My cock twitched in his mouth as I savored the warmth while I gently tugged on his hair. He was in control, and dear God, he could do whatever he wanted to me.

"Fuck...Jack...aaah..." He stopped to bite gently on my hip following down to my thigh. His eyes were closed, but that expression on his face. Blissful. At peace. The first time I had ever seen him something other than some flavor of upset or annoyed. Something pulled my eyes away to look at the clock on the stove across the living room. 12:56am. Already? And Seven Minutes in Heaven felt like an hour back in middle school.

"Bedroom?" Jack purred, turning those Bambi eyes up at me. Was he a mind reader?

"Anywhere you want." I sighed. Couch? Floor? You name it. Jack could have said behind the dumpster at Helena's and I would have gone with him. Romantic, I know. As he stood he took my hand, gently tucking his hair behind his ears with the other. That's when I noticed the white scars that danced up and down his arms, front and back. They intersected and collided looking like the spiderwebs of a car windshield after a wreck. Jack caught me looking and quickly wrapped his long fingers around his upper arms in a poor attempt to prevent the sleeves from riding up more. Pink flushed across his cheeks before spreading down and under his shirt.

"I..." Jack bit his lip and looked away. For the first time, Jack did not flinch away from my hand as I gently grabbed his jaw, pulled his face towards mine and kissed him. One step after another, I steered him towards the bedroom, which was past the kitchen and across the living room, never breaking our kiss.

1:08am read the stove.

Clothes quickly slid off once we were in the bedroom. Hands groped and grabbed wanting to explore every part. Lips followed fingers and breath hot against skin. We were entangled in each other leaving no spot of bare skin unexplored by touch or mouth.

Even in the dark of the room, as I forgot to turn the light on, I could see his scars expanded far beyond just his arms. Across his pale thighs, stomach, hips, even his back. Thin lines occasionally broken with large, thick, keloid scars. Some of those scars were the size of Jack's fingers which lay beside one in an attempt to cover them from view. So many stories, with probably just as many sources gauging by the deep marks on Jack's back. Acid hit the back of my throat at what might have caused those deep, almost claw-like marks.

"I'm sorry..." Jack whispered before slowly moving his hands and folding them tightly in his lap. His eyes were closed, like he was afraid of looking at me. From my spot, kneeling before him on the floor, I could tell he was ashamed of his scars. I buried my face between his thighs and kissed each one. My hands found his and I looked up at him, his face blurry above my glasses.

"You're beautiful." I kissed his thighs again before gently pushing him back onto the bed. My hands slid up his stomach to lovingly caress the scars there. Moving to sit on the edge of my bed, I pulled Jack into my lap. His warmth flooded over me. I groaned and buried my face in his hair. The smell of smoke and lemon filled my nose. He was mine. Even if it was just for this night, he was all mine.

"Jack..." I said breathlessly. He slowly

reached up, grabbing my chin in his hands. Searching for something, anything in my eyes. The sound of our breathing filled the vacuum that had been created around us. Despite being of average build I felt so large while I had Jack like this against me. My fingers gently explored his back, tracing the scars there. Along his shoulder blades and back down his spine. Shivering, Jack tilted his head and kissed me. His black hair was a mess, but it still managed to look like it was done on purpose. There was a softness in the way he gazed upon me.

It was my turn to tease as I did the exact thing Jack had done to me earlier. He moaned into the kiss, tongue pressing hard against mine. His hips rocked into my hand, caressing and stroking him. Something caught the light from the ajar door. Black barbells through each of Jack's nipples. How had I not noticed them before? I growled and felt Jack tense under my hand. Up across his stomach my hands slid and to his nipples to gently tug on the metal. The response was instant, and loud, causing me to whine in need. Every sound Jack made only served to make me more desperate.

Reaching over Jack's shoulder and to my nightstand, I fumbled in the drawer. His skin was hot and wet against mine due to being slick with sweat. Before I realized, Jack had taken the condom from my hands and opened it with his teeth. Delicately, he slid it over my cock before pushing me backwards and climbing on me. Each bony hip was marked with a black rose, petals spread to show red deep at the roots.

"Guess I got to see them, huh?" Jack went to dismount and I grabbed his arm, laughing. "Sorry, sorry." Jack smiled softly and I realized he had said almost nothing this whole time. Red numbers flipped over to 1:49am. Less than an hour. There wouldn't be time. If Jack knew the time, he didn't care as he climbed back on top of me. While I had been worrying about the time, Jack had grabbed the lube from my nightstand. The viscous liquid dripped from his hands as he made sure we were both ready. I reached around grabbing his ass in my hands and feeling a hungry growl rumble in my chest.

My groping fingers grabbed at Jack's as I brushed his hand aside, sliding a finger into him. His eyelids fluttered and a moan passed his lips. His back arched and I ran a finger down his chest and stomach, feeling his muscles tense around and under me.

"Jack-" I tried to warn him about the time. My worry causing me to become soft. Could I perform under this pressure? A thought that left my mind quick as a dry finger pressed to my lips as the other hand was wiped unceremoniously on my bed.

"I know. I don't care." Jack moaned as I slid his finger past my lips, letting it graze across my teeth. "I want this..." He whined the words. God, I wanted him too. No, I needed him *now*.

Wrapping my hands around Jack's hips, I slowly lowered him onto my cock. Leaning over, he kissed me with a passion matched by only my own. He needed this as much as I did. Guided by my over-sized hands, his hips moved in rhythm with mine. Once more our tongues explored each other's mouths. Our teeth collided occasionally with my thrusts, but neither of us seemed to mind. I could kiss him for hours, I thought as I felt his teeth tug gently on my lower lip. Spit caught in the pale light causing his chin to glisten. Our moans and gasps were the only thing that broke that kiss as passionate sounds filled the room.

Being careful not to crush him underneath me, we moved together so that I was over him. His legs wrapped around my waist with his heels digging almost painfully into my lower back. My fingers curled around his cock and I moved in rhythm with my own thrusts. I lost myself watching Jack's body writhe in pleasure under me. Fistfuls of sheets were tugged on in ecstasy. Jack's back arched and pressed him into both my hips and my hand. I was getting close.

“Cum for me.” I whispered harshly into Jack’s ear, pulling his earlobe between my teeth. Jack’s moan echoed in the bedroom as his back arched sharply to press against me. A high-pitched whine hissed from between his teeth and into my ear. “Cum for me.” I repeated as I felt Jack’s cock twitch in my grasp.

As I straightened up for a better angle, my hips slapping harder and faster against Jack, he came. His body shuddered and tensed around me with his orgasm splashing across his stomach and chest. I didn’t last longer after, the whines and moans of his orgasm and rhythmic clenching pushing me over the edge. I wasn’t done with him yet. Bending down, I dragged my tongue along his stomach and chest savoring the salt of his sweat and cum. My tongue teased his nipples and he squealed, pushing me away with a blush that turned his entire chest and shoulders red.

“S-sensitive.” Jack stammered between panted breaths. Slowly and reluctantly, I pulled myself from Jack and went to lay beside him when the red glow of the clock brought me crashing back to reality. 2:46am. Fuck. Fuck. *FUCK*. So much for savoring the afterglow.

We were lucky we didn’t get pulled over,

driving like maniacs at almost 3am. We had a hard time limit and couldn't risk the consequences. Jack didn't say a word the entire drive. What was he thinking? I wanted to ask but the look on his face said I shouldn't.

As I pulled up to Helena's I could see Jack shaking in his seat. I knew what he was afraid of and it was a fear we shared.

"It's ok." I said, kissing him softly. Those dark Bambi eyes were filled with fear. What if Gideon was here early? What if someone said something? He didn't need to say the questions for me to know they were spinning around his head as well as so many more. "It'll be ok, I promise." I kissed his forehead. With that he opened the door and before leaving turned to look at me, tears running down his face.

"Thank you." He smiled and walked through the doors of the bar. The drive back home was quiet and warm.

V.

I kept waiting for another call that never came. Asking for another night at my place and another round. Going out for a date or drinks somewhere fancier than Helena's for a real night out. Hell, maybe something more stating he was leaving Gideon for me. These thoughts may have been outlandish fantasies, but I couldn't shake them and they were better than where my mind would go if I didn't try to stay positive.

There was always the opposite possibilities too. Gideon calling and stating that he knew. Or even worse, Jack calling me in tears, upset and hurt, because of what we had done. His scars haunted me. Absolutely no way that they were all self-inflicted. Hell, some of the ones on his back looked like the types of scars you would see in history books; the deep cutting scars of a whip. What kind of monster was Gideon Bellview? And more importantly, how could I save Jack? These thoughts consumed me as I thought of every outcome.

To make sure I didn't accidentally run into Gideon again I avoided Helena's for a bit. I kept my phone on me at all times – waiting. Expecting a call from either Jack or Gideon. Anxiety ripped through me every night, worried I would sleep through a desperate call from Jack and be too late. Too late? Christ, would it come to that? Eventually, it got to be too much. Jack wasn't calling and I was worried. Too scared to dare call his phone myself, I made my way to Helena's.

"JUDAH!" All I had done was open the door to the place and Jack was stomping towards me. How did he know it was me? His hands were curled into fists so tight that his knuckles were a stark white. If his nails were any longer I'm sure his palms would be bleeding. Blinking in confusion, I lifted my hands in a plea.

"Jack, hey uh...wha-" Jack's fist collided with my chest. I grunted and took a step back into the outside as the sharp pain radiated across my chest and I gasped for breath. He was small, but he had focused his punch right to my solar plexus. A hush came over the bar that muted everything including the music that had seemed so loud only moments ago. Over Jack's head I could see the others in the bar staring at us.

"Fuck. You." Another hit to my chest and he stormed past me through the door. So much for an excited hello, how are you? Where have you been?

And more hopefully, I missed you.

"Jack, wait!" I stumbled after him, panting and confused. "Seriously, wait!" I shouted. Jack sat on the bench out front of the bar with his face buried in his hands. His shoulders shook in sobbing motions. I could hear the hiccuping in the dead silence of the cold night. While a busy road during the day, once the evening commute was over, it was dead. A road meant for nothing more than getting in and out of city which explained why there were three other bars on the same stretch.

Standing outside the bar, I realized how cold it was. I shivered and could see Jack's breath coming out in small clouds like he had just ran a mile. Across the street, the donut shop's sign matched even Helena's in its disrepair. The combination convenience store and gas station next store blazed brightly. The brightness seemed out of place, especially compared to the dinginess that Rio's Donuts and Helena's brought to the street. A safe haven for travelers, though this time of night there would be no one until the drunks stumbled from the bars. They would stop to fill up their cars and stomachs on their way home from a night out to celebrate, drown their sorrows, or get lucky. A desperate attempt to sober up with coffee and food before driving into a waiting cop car that always sat down the road.

"Jack, I-" What was I even apologizing for? The bench creaked under my weight as I sat next to Jack. Waiting for any hint as to what I had done or what had happened. Oh god, what had happened? My heart sank and I felt sick to my stomach. What pain and suffering had our transgression caused Jack?

"Go away." Jack hiccuped. Slowly, I placed a hand on his shoulder which he wiggled out from under.

"Why? I don't-" Panicked. "You have to tell me what I did, Jack..." Those eyes glared at me from behind his fingers, looking like black pits when compared to his fair skin.

"Men like you..." He spit on the ground and said something in French.

"I don't understand..." I attempted to reach out again. Jack didn't try to move away this time, but that stare held me with his eyes flickering under the street lights.

"You got what you wanted. Fuck off now." Jack snarled.

"Is Gideon making you do this?" Apparently this was funny to Jack. A cruel, harsh laugh caused him to pull his hands away and cover his mouth. His sleeves moved to reveal fresh red marks on his wrists. Where they from Gideon? I suddenly felt sick.

"Really? Gideon? Judah, please." He placed a hand on my thigh before he stood, fishing a cigarette out of his bag. He lit it, took a long drag, closing his eyes before letting the smoke roll from between his lips. "You really have no idea?" He sounded amused.

"No, I really don't." Never had I felt so lost, so stupid. There was something going on and apparently I was staring at it, completely unable to comprehend it.

"You fuck me and then I don't hear from you or see you for what, a week? Two weeks?" He took another drag, free hand clenching and unclenching. "What am I supposed to think?"

"I was trying to keep distance. So Gideon wouldn't..." I rubbed my face and sighed deeply. "With all those scars and the fight last time, I thought that maybe if he found out...something bad would happen."

"You think those scars are from Gideon?" Jack laughed again, he sounded like a jackal. Sharp. Manic. "You really are fucking stupid."

Those words hit hard. Sure, I wasn't the best

at human interaction, but I meant no ill will. I just wanted to keep Jack safe. I just wanted to protect him. I had already seen what type of person Gideon was. There was no way I could know what he was truly capable of. But to call me stupid? After I had put myself on the line too?

"I saw how he acted at the bar. The bruise on your face. How afraid of him you are." I felt so small sitting next to Jack like this.

"You don't know anything. We've met what, less than five times? We fuck and suddenly you know everything about me and my life?" Jack crushed the butt under his boot heel. Turning to look at me, he rolled his lip between his teeth. A nervous reaction. Something he did when he was mulling over what to say next.

"I know he's abusive. I know you have scars on your back." Jack lit another cigarette as I spoke, eyes turned away from me.

"Judah. Those scars are from my family." He sat heavily next to me, handing the cigarette towards me. I took it and took a long, deep drag from it. The smoke burned my lungs. I held it until my eyes burned and I coughed when those words left Jack's lips. "I have a lot to still tell you about my family. There is a reason I saw Gideon as my knight in shining armor, why we got married so fast..." Jack sighed.

"I'm sorry..." I placed my hand on Jack's thigh again, squeezing gently. He let out a small yelp, swatting my hand away. "Sorry..." I mumbled again.

"As you know, my family is Catholic. But I mean, *really* Catholic. I told them I was gay at the age of 16 and after that they tried to exorcise the demons from me." Jack sneered. "It sounds all so cliché. But really, they thought I was possessed. They blamed everything they could. The media, music, even the Catholic school I went to. Everyone but themselves and their genetics." I watched as Jack smoked the rest of the cigarette in silence. That's how we sat there, watching as snow began to fall and dance in the street light. Total silence.

"Judah..." Jack spoke softly, placing his fingers over my hand. "I'm sorry." His apology caught me off guard.

"No, I should be the one apologizing." I squeezed his hand, scooting closer as I noticed a shiver run through his body. "I shouldn't have assumed anything."

"No, but you're right. Gideon is abusive." Speaking the words out loud seemed to catch Jack off guard. His thumb rubbed the top of my hand until it was red. I didn't move it even though it was starting to get a bit painful. There were a million emotions swimming in those eyes.

"It's ok." I squeezed his hand again before wrapping my arm around his shoulders. Jack felt small underneath my arm. Smaller than usual. No, he felt frail. Delicate like even the weight of my arm alone would crush him. He didn't push me away, he just looked at me pitifully.

"It's not ok. I'm not ok." He buried his face into his hands again, and I pulled him against me. His body shook with a sob and I could feel his tears on my shirt. I refused to move. Jack would be the one to lead the way with what he wanted. I was an idiot who didn't know how to read him, he was right about that. How do you handle this type of situation? What could someone like me offer to Jack?

"Whatever you need." Murmuring into his ear, I kissed the top of his head. My face buried into his soft black hair, which was already down for once.

"What I need is for you to not leave again." Jack stated flatly.

"I never left in the first place." I said.

Jack squirmed from under me, lip pulled back in utter disgust. He looked repulsed by me like

I had in the span of seconds went from normal person to the *Creature from the Black Lagoon.* Something horrific and slimy.

"You wouldn't call that leaving?" He hissed the words, grabbing his bag from the sidewalk. "What did you do then? What would you call that?" His tone was raising, voice becoming shrill. Water filled his eyes and those long, dark lashes broke the dam.

"I gave you space! I protected you! I-" Had I really done those things? I fell silent. Jack was right. I didn't try to call. We had fucked and then I essentially ghosted him.

"You vanished and I thought I would never see you again! I felt so stupid for thinking you wanted something other than sex. I trusted you!" Blood ran down Jack's chin as he bit his lip. His nostrils flared as tears spilled in unstoppable waves down his cheeks. All to familiar black rivers. By this point I half expected the door of Helena's to open and the bartender to look out. A black car with blacked out windows drove by slowly trying to rubberneck our fight. So much for trying to be discreet.

Without another word, Jack rolled up his sleeves showing the bright, angry red that crossed along his arms. Both arms had new wounds, some scabbed over while others seemed ready to bleed at a moments notice. Thin and precise. “Really?” He whispered. “Is that really what you think you did Judah? You really think you didn’t just fuck me and then ditch me for days, no call, no text?”

“I didn’t want-” I stammered.

“Gideon to find out?” Jack finished, snarkily. “Sure.” Jack yanked his sleeves back down. “Those are all because of you. You did this.” Jack turned on his heel and stormed off, face contorting in a mix of emotions. Rage. Pain. Betrayal. I could identify them all as the car door slamming echoed through out the cold and nearly empty lot. Silently, I watched as his car screeched out of the parking lot and down the road, red taillights fading from sight. There was nothing more I wanted to do than to chase his car down that long road. I wanted to scream and yell and apologize. Again. And again. And again. Like I had so many times already. Instead, I had stayed silent and let him walk away.

My scream was echoing across the parking lot before I even realized what I was doing. Throwing a fit like a child, I let it all out until my throat was raw and hoarse. The cold air burned my lungs as I panted and heaved. I banged on the metal bench until my fists would be black, blue and red. Fuck. Fuck. Fuck. Tears ran down my face and I smudged my own blood through my hair, pulling on giant fistfuls. Fuck. *FUCK.*

A gentle tap came and I spun, hand cocked and connecting with something. No, *someone*. The bartender stood his ground as my fist connected with his chest. While I was big, he was even bigger. Dual role of bouncer and bartender with that build. Air wheezed into my lungs as he plucked my fist from his chest and I let it fall limply.

"Go home." He said, pointing to the parking lot. Several curious bystanders looked like curious little raccoons, peering from around the door held ajar. "Leave. You're disturbing the peace." He spoke sternly.

So I left.

VI.

Without Jack, I felt lost. No, more than lost. I felt vacant. Days bleed into just some mishmash of colors and sounds that slip by and through your fingers like water, or in my case, alcohol. When your mind loses its sense of purpose, it loses its sense of time or shape or matter. A plastic bag drifting where the wind takes it. You have nowhere to call home, no corporeal form to tie you to the world around you. Just discarded garbage.

I called Jack the night after our fight. Immediately to voicemail. Not sure what I was expecting, but it stung just the same. Words poured from my mouth until the harsh beep and automated message brought me crashing back down. Yes, I would like to delete the message. Another, but different, beep as I dropped my phone onto my night stand. The red numbers on my alarm seemed brighter and harsher then they did before. Too much like the neon sign at Helena's that illuminated Jack like some type of cyberpunk angel.

Everything brought me back to that fight. Every word that was said, every movement that each of us took. Each day caused my gut to twist and turn, a constant anxiety about what was to come. Walking past the smokers at work brought flashbacks to those big, hurt eyes. The way Jack held his cigarette between his pursed lips, trying not to smash the filter in his distress. His whole body seemed to vibrate, not from the cold, but from trying to keep everything in. A bottle shaken and ready to burst, regardless of how delicately one tried to open it.

Helena's offered no respite. The nights I was able to slip by the bartender, Jack was never there. No one had seen him, but I really don't think they would have told me if they had anyway. They all had not only heard the fight, but seen it too. Those faces all peeking around the door to gossip among themselves long after they had left for the night. Gossip I heard in bits and pieces as I returned to Helena's with a shaky truce with the bartender. He kept me company on those long, lonely nights going as far as to tell me that the bar was started by his grandfather and named after his grandmother. Our conversations were brief, but I appreciated the attempts to quell the turmoil in my mind with something other than the alcohol.

I called again. And again. And again. I tried to call at all hours of the day. Maybe Jack had a day job? Maybe his phone was dead? Maybe, he didn't want to see my sorry ass again. I was desperate, to say the least. Hopefully Jack hadn't saved my number under my name and if he had, be damned with the consequences. I had to apologize. There could at least be no accusations of lack of effort this time.

I chased down all the bars along that strip of road too. Taking some nights to wait it out at Cocky's, Gabe's, and The Haven, with no luck. None of them had the same feel or atmosphere of Helena's. These were the bars you saw in movies and on TV shows with loud music, crowded bodies, and drinks with clever names. All bright neon glow and sweat. Yet somehow, everyone was noticed in those places. Too much attention. There was no way Jack would come to one of these places, right? It was during these searches I realized how little I actually knew about Jack.

A few conversations here and there never reveals the full picture. It never could. Jack's words, "we fuck and suddenly you know everything about me" echoed in my mind. Yet, there was that forever nagging feeling in my guts when I was in those places. Jack wore a lot about him on his sleeve, quite literally. He talked openly and freely about his past and his opinions, but his current life? That I knew nothing about. Besides his marriage to Gideon. Even then, I only knew bits and pieces. His interests, whether or not he had a job, his hobbies, I knew none of it. I returned to my post at Helena's, hoping that my gut was right. Jack would show up again, hopefully. If not, then...I didn't want to think about that. He had shown back up before and there was something that pulled at my heart that Jack was a creature of habit. Plus, someone just doesn't keep coming back to a bar where no one talks to them for no reason. Jack *had* to come back at some point. When? That was the big question.

"Hello?" I groggily answered the phone, rubbing my eyes and staring at my clock. 4:00am exactly. Sleep held down my anger at being awoken, smothering it under a pillow for now. The clock clicked over to the next minute before the voice answered on the other end.

"Judah?" Jack questioned timidly. His voice was distance and tinny; a bad connection. I checked my phone to confirm but UNKNOWN CALLER displayed across the screen. There was no question though, that the voice with the hard but strained accent on the other end belonged to Jack.

"Jack? Is that you?" Loud static pulled me more from my sleep causing any anger to quickly dissipate. "Can you hear me?" More static.

"Yes, it's me. Judah, I need to see you. Helena's. Tomorrow. I'll explain everything." The words were quick and quiet, and I almost missed half of what he said because of the static. He was clipping in and out, almost like he was trying to call from inside a tunnel. "Judah? Did you hear me?" Jack whispered.

"I'm here. Tomorrow. Helena's." Click. No goodbye, no other confirmation. I stared at the disconnected phone, displaying CALL ENDED. Was I dreaming? It felt and sounded like Jack was calling from a dream. It would account for the bad connection and the static. A ghost in the wire. But why so late? If Jack was truly a ghost, then the timing made sense. You don't hear about ghost stories occurring in the middle of the day. That's when I realized that Gideon probably went to bed at 4am, soon after Jack would be getting home from the 3am last call of Helena's. Had I somehow missed Jack? The thought made me sick.

Sleep did not come back to me nor did I try. The anxiety bubbling in my stomach would take at least another hour or two to calm down. My alarm would go off for work in three hours anyway. I showered, I cleaned, I did anything to make the hours pass quicker. I don't remember driving to my job. Work disappeared in such a blur that I'm still not sure if I actually did anything productive. There was only one thing on my mind, and it was getting to Helena's.

I arrived as early as I possibly could. The door felt heavier than usual as I pushed it open into the dark interior that made up Helena's. There was a strange tension in the air. Something didn't sit right as I looked around the bar. The music seemed quieter, almost somber. There were only a few people besides the bartender. Sadness. There was a sadness that hung in the air, a quiet loneliness that lurked in every shadow of the place. Every bar stool seemed to be covered in a layer of darkness, devouring even the bright neon lights of the signs along the walls. It felt more like a wake than a bar.

Nestling into my place and ordering a whiskey to ease my nerves, even the bartender – whose name I still hadn't bothered to learn – seemed to be moving at half speed. My lack of sleep must have been catching up to me. The adrenaline of making it through the day was wearing off. I sipped my drink and waited keeping that heavy and dark door at the corner of my eye. Despite my best efforts, and with the help of the alcohol, I could feel my eyelids getting heavier.

Minutes slipped by like hours. Everything felt like a heavy breath, clawing to be released and yet held back, blocked by something. Suffocating in weight and volume. At some point I passed out. I wasn't the first person to fall asleep at the bar, and as with anyone else, I was left alone. Minutes finally free to pass as slow or fast as they wanted to in my unconscious state.

"Hey..." A soft voice woke me with a shake. Grumbling, I swatted the offending hand only to be greeted with an even stronger shake. "How many drinks did you have?" A short pause. "Only one? Huh." I could hear Jack pursing his lips as he gave me another shake.

"I'm up." I growled and that gentle hand slipped from my shoulder. As my eyes adjusted to the lack of light, I realized that Jack was sitting to my left as opposed to my right as he normally did. Every shadow clung heavily to his slight frame, obscuring almost every detail from me, but especially his face. My frame blocked any pink glow that usually enveloped him as I sat up. "I'm up." I stated again, wiping the crust from the corners of my eyes. Christ, how long had I been out?

"We need to talk," Jack said. His hands fidgeted in his lap and he worked over his lower lip with his teeth.

"Let me just say...I'm sorry. I'm not the greatest at..." I let my words fall. What did I mean?

Greatest at what? This wasn't a relationship. Friendship? What did we have? I let the words echo and end with a shrug.

Jack nodded. He licked his lips, black lipstick having rubbed off on his front teeth from the anxious gnawing. It made his teeth looked chipped and broken.

"I've been thinking." Jack raised his hand to stop me before I could interject. "Just let me finish." A sigh deep enough I could see his chest press against his shirt. "I've been thinking. A lot. About us, whatever it is we have, whatever you want to call," his hands flailed openly in the air, "this."

"I feel safe with you, Judah." He continued. The word safe seemed pained, the opposite of what it should. "I don't feel so alone with you." Jack's hand found mine and he squeezed them. There was fear in his eyes, but a different fear than I was used to. This wasn't the fear of someone, as it had been in the past. This was the type of fear of change, but tinged with something else – hope.

"Jack, what are you saying?" The words burned as they came out. I had been holding my breath the whole time Jack spoke. My throat and mouth were dry. I glanced at my glass, but it was empty.

"I want to try." Jack looked up as he spoke. Those big doe eyes sparkled underneath heavy black eyelashes. Truly sparkled, and not from the reflection of any of the lights around us.

"Try?" Air rushed into my chest, and continued to fill me to an almost painful level. My insides knotted and twisted. My heart slammed in my throat. I knew what Jack was saying, but some level of me wasn't ready to accept it yet.

"Judah, I can't do it anymore." Jack's voice didn't falter. There was a confidence that I hadn't seen before, especially when it came to speaking of his relationship with Gideon.

"Are you sure this is smart? What if-" I said before Jack cut me off.

"I don't care!" He roared, squeezing my hands hard enough that I could feel his nails threaten to break my skin. "Damn it all!" When he realized everyone was staring, he lowered his head. "I deserve to be happy." He whispered to the room.

"Why not just leave?" I asked. A simple enough question that received daggers from Jack.

"He'll kill me." The words were spat out, like a spoiled piece of meat someone had chewed on for far too long. Slimy and full of sinew. Something that would not be broken down, no matter how long you tried. Full of disgust, contempt, and worst of all, deception.

"He'll kill you if he finds out." I pleaded.

"At least...at least I would have been happy for a bit." Jack sighed, running those needle fingers through his hair and pulling on the ends. It hung freely tonight, a perfect veil to obscure his reactions to me and to the rest of the bar.

Such words held great sorrow. I couldn't deny Jack his escape. What may be his only attempt to escape. From the corner of my eye I could see the bartender watching us while pretending to wash an empty glass. Was I being paranoid? Did Gideon have spies everywhere in the bar? There was no way. Gideon would already know about Jack and I if that were the case. As much as we thought we were being sneaky, we were the exact opposite.

"Why now?" I had to know what had spurred this revelation on. Jack falls silent and disappears for days only to return with this plan. What happened? I swallowed hard and tried to keep down the unease that was rising inside of me. There was no need to jump to awful conclusions now.

"Gideon leaves for China for a month. If all goes well, it could be even longer." Jack chewed on his lip again. He disappeared for a second, those eyes growing vacant in a daydream. He shook his head before continuing, “It’s now or never. Judah, do you understand that?”

Of course I understood that. Jack would be left alone. We’d have all the time to do whatever we wanted so that Gideon would never know. No worry about him dropping by suddenly or time limits we had to abide by. Freedom to do what we wanted, when we wanted, how we wanted. A smile crept across my face that I couldn’t contain. No more sneaking around like grounded teenagers.

“Plus, he broke my phone cause it kept ringing.” Jack sipped on his drink which had materialized in front of him. I could feel his gaze on me as he waited for me to understand the implications of his words. I felt my whole body turn red in embarrassment. “He thinks I’ll be cut off while he’s gone.” Jack chuckled before pulling out another phone from his bag. It was a simple pay-as-you-go phone. That would explain why he had come up as UNKNOWN CALLER. His calls were no longer being tied to Gideon.

“No more robocalls at all hours of the day.” I hissed through clenched teeth and Jack laughed. A genuine, full body laugh. It bounced and echoed through out the bar, floating above the music and noise of the bar. That odd and sorrowful feeling was chased away by the sound.

“He leaves on Monday.” Jack finished his drink and smiled softly at me. Leaning forward he kissed me gently and floated out that door. Hopefully, one of the last times we would have to use the cover of alcohol and dim lights. Well, I guess I had a boyfriend now?

The bartender was squinting at me as I looked away from the door Jack had just left through. Due to the light it was hard to tell if it was bewilderment or if he was judging us for the conversation he just overheard. I waved him over and he turned his back to me. So much for hospitality. Switching seats and loudly coughing caused him to turn and before he could try and ignore me again, I spoke. “Let’s try something new tonight. What mixed drinks can you make?” I grinned as the bartender rolled his eyes at me.

VII.

Getting ready for Monday went quicker than I expected. We still had our meetings at Helena's but there was a heaviness there. A fire blanket, meant to smother our excitement as we dared not make too many plans in the open. Despite the safety that the bar seemed to offer we couldn't be too sure who was listening or watching. We were too close now to risk it. There was a whole month of plans to be made and it all felt like a house of cards. Any wrong move would bring it all toppling down on our heads.

Jack and I spoke nightly on the phone (always past 4am) in hushed tones about our aspirations. It somehow felt safer than Helena's. Gideon was a loud sleeper. Maybe not the brightest idea but we were excited. Acting like two high school sweethearts despite being well past that age. I think some part of us hoped that if we got caught it would be now before there was any real danger to what we were planning. We talked about where we wanted to go, what we wanted to do and how to proceed once our month long love affair ended.

- VII. -

Jack wanted to do so many different things while we were together. He wanted to go out to eat and go to the movies. He especially wanted to go to the recently renovated aquarium he had been begging Gideon to take him to for months. For me, I wanted to look at apartments, jobs for the both of us, and ways to bring our lives together. Support ourselves away from this awful city. Moving from Georgia, I didn't really have much choice. I picked wherever I could find a job and a place then moved. Clearly it wasn't working out for neither Jack nor I. Jack wanted to stay in a city at one point, suggesting New York. My laughing response got me an annoyed tongue click over the phone. Too many people, too expensive, and too close.

We had to cram an entire courtship into one month. One month to figure out if this was going to work. So many different aspects to see if we were truly compatible. It was a lot, to say the least. None of it seemed to scare Jack though. He talked openly and eagerly about all of his plans. When we met at Helena's, his mood was clearly happier. There was a bounce to his step and while I loved it, it also made me worry. Would Gideon notice this complete change in demeanor? Jack assured me that was not the case as he spent most of his time at work now – preparing for his trip out of the country.

As Monday drew closer my mind wouldn't stop racing. Plans were finally being set into motion. There was this growing pit in my stomach over the whole situation. What if Gideon canceled? What if he came back early? What if he bugged the house and knew Jack was out all day? What if, what if, what if? Every scenario ran through my head, no matter how dark the outcome.

"Jack, are you sure about this?" I whispered into the phone on Saturday night.

"I've made up my mind." Jack stated plainly.

"But-"

"No buts, Judah. Either you're in this with me or you're not." Jack's voice wavered at the mere thought. My heart broke. Jack deserved so much more than Gideon could ever give him.

"Aw sugar, of course I'm with you." A Southern twang crept forth and Jack laughed.

"Excuse me?" He was still laughing.

"Sorry. I was born in Georgia, ya know." I sighed. No matter how much I tried, something always managed to bring those memories back.

"No, no. It's cute," Jack chuckled. "I'll talk to you tomorrow."

"Is it Monday yet?" I whined, not wanting the call to end yet despite how tired I was.

"No," Jack sighed. "Not yet."

"Soon." I said.

"Soon." Jack repeated before hanging up.

Going to bed after our conversations were always hard. My brain took so long to wind down and the butterflies in my stomach were surely actually moths. It meant I barely got any sleep before heading into work and would sneak naps in the bathroom here and there in order to function. How I never crashed my car still surprises me as there were more than a few drives to and from work that I do not remember. And yet, the days leading up to Monday marched forward.

~~~~~~~~~~~~~~~~~~~~~~~~~~~

When Monday came Gideon left early in the morning. That left Jack the whole day to spend digging through the mansion to try and find any trace of a camera, a wire, anything that would say Gideon was onto us. He had never done it before, but Jack had also never planned on leaving Gideon; there was a first time for everything. When we
~~~~~~~~~~~~~~~~~~~~~~~~~~~

decided the coast was clear, we met at Helena's for what would hopefully be the last time. It was bittersweet, the thought of never having to walk through that door again. At the same time I could feel myself slipping into bad habits I thought I had left behind so maybe it was for the better.

Jack's plan was a simple one. He would leave before me and I would wait here for a little bit. Make it look like Jack had left to go home and then I would go home myself a little bit after. Not exactly the best plan, but after hours on the phone, I couldn't come up with anything better. Jack had checked the mansion for bugs and came up empty-handed. And no one came knocking after I had brought Jack home either, so we didn't think anyone was following us around. It would look like Jack left to go home, I got bored after Jack left (per usual) and then I went home myself.

I slipped my key into Jack's hand watching as he curled his fingers over the cold metal. My heart flung itself into my throat. The words burned. They were so hard to get out. The risk we were taking. I swallowed hard, gasping for air. In the darkness of Helena's I could see that Jack was clutching my key so tightly his knuckles were white. Was he having second thoughts?

"One hour." Those two simple words felt like

acid bubbling from my lips. Jack simply nodded and went back to sipping his drink. We idly chatted. Jack pretended to check his phone, wished me goodnight, and left. I felt like everyone was staring at me. My skin crawled with their all-knowing gaze. Could they see through the ruse? Why were we making this such a big deal here now? At no point before had our secrets left the confines of Helena's, so why did we think they would now? Surely anything that had been said or done would have already reached Gideon and damned us long ago.

Despite being a Monday, or because of, the bar was packed. So many prying eyes that could potentially ruin the plan. Jack and I had been careful though, there was no reason for Gideon to assume anything, and thus, no need for spies. Soon I would go back to my apartment, Jack already waiting for me, and we would give it a shot. One month to see if we could make this work, make it worth the risk we we daring to take. Not enough time, but we had no choice. Jack's confidence in the situation usually calmed my worries, but for now I was left alone with my own thoughts.

All I could think about was how much longer I had until I could go home. Until I could see Jack. Until I could be with Jack. Be with...Jack. It was official, Jack was mine. For now anyway. An unfamiliar warmth crept through me, pressing my heart into both my throat and my stomach. I smiled to myself and took a sip of my drink. I felt like a balloon that was floating away – light and free. My eyes floated over to the bartender who was staring intently at me. There was no attempt to hide his gaze. The way he was staring made my insides go cold and sink, deflating hard and fast. The bartender shook his head and turned away, moving to help a new face that had just sat down at the bar with a companion whose mouth was moving a mile a minute.

By the time the halfway mark hit, I could feel the knots destroying my guts. Doubt was starting to creep in again. Was Jack's plan as new or as randomly Heaven-sent as I had originally thought? How many other attempts had there been? I buried my face in my hands after draining my drink and let my mind go. Every possible scenario, every possible outcome, both good and bad. I let it wash over me and surrendered myself to the waves. Helena's melted away as my mind raced. Not even the music could reach me here. Now I knew where Jack went when those eyes looked so distant, reaching and searching for an escape. Any possible plan or idea that would take him away from his life and situation. Except, I wasn't looking for an escape. I was looking for an answer. I couldn't bring this negativity home with me. I wouldn't let it taint my time with Jack.

My phone buzzed and pulled me back into the bar. Sound rushed back into my head, causing me to grit my teeth against the onslaught and headache that it brought. Go time. The walk through the bar felt like walking through zero gravity. My feet barely touched the floor. I was floating. I pushed the door open and stepped into the outside, the night was bright and clear. I took a deep breath, feeling the cool air burn its way down my sinuses and into my lungs. Now or never.

Walking into my own apartment felt wrong. Everything felt forbidden, like it wasn't my apartment anymore – an alternate dimension. Turning the key, the deadbolt echoed through out the courtyard and I felt my chest grow tight. I realized I had been holding my breath as I opened the door into the darkness. This was not what I had been expecting. I had expected that the lights would all be on with Jack sitting on the couch and waiting for me. Or raiding my fridge. Something full of light and life, not this heavy darkness that blanketed the entire apartment in a thick and oppressive silence. The only thing I could hear was the click of the clock above my TV, a cat whose eyes and tail moved with the ticking seconds.

"Jack?" I called out softly, half expecting someone else to answer. Had Jack's nerves gotten the best of him? Did he realize on the drive over that this was a stupid idea? Did he drive past and go off to start his new life alone? I hung my keys on the hook next to the door, shutting it behind me and throwing the deadbolt. Inside of the apartment, the noise rang hollow and empty. There was no sense of life besides my own here. Goose bumps shot up my arms.

"Jack?" I called again, louder this time. No response. I clicked the lights on and looked over on the couch. Empty. Not even a jacket or Jack's bag to show that at least he was or had been here. The bathroom door stood wide open, the dim glow of the nightlight showing no hidden intruders either. Something caught in my throat as I struggled to swallow. A joke? Not Jack's sense of humor and definitely not funny.

Only one door lay closed still; the bedroom. No light rushed from under the door and there was no sound or movement from behind it. Still better to check before letting utter despair take over. Right? Turning the doorknob slowly, as to not startle any potential intruders, I glanced in. There I saw Jack laying on my bed. His hair spilled out under him looking like blood it was so dark and shiny against the sheets. His chest rose and fell softly and his mouth was slightly open as he snored so gently my ears strained to hear it. He had passed out on top of the sheets with his bag dropped next to the bed with its contents strewn across the floor.

Jack slowly awoke as I sat down next to him on the bed. My weight caused the bed to creak and Jack rolled towards me. He mumbled something before curling up against my back.

"Your shoes are still on." I chuckled. Jack didn't move. He returned to snoring softly. Silently, I rose from the bed and Jack weakly pawed at me in his sleep. His eyes never opened nor did he stir much more as I removed his shoes and wrapped him in the sheets. There were a few things I had to do for work before I could follow Jack into bed. A smile crossed my lips and I sighed. It all felt so natural already and Jack clearly felt comfortable enough to immediately walk in and pass out. Or he was just exhausted and relieved to finally be without Gideon for a short while.

Quietly, I made myself a cup of tea and settled into my work desk. My back was to the rest of the living room, a purposeful design to avoid watching the TV while I had work to do. Did this always stop me from procrastinating while things like YouTube existed and I had two monitors? Of course not, but I liked to pretend that it did. I didn't bother to turn on the living room lights either, the glow of the screens was enough for me. Probably bad for my eyes if my glasses were any indication. The work I had to do was minimal, just putting some numbers into an Excel spreadsheet and tidying it up. Work, that was supposed to be done a week ago, but I had been too wrapped up in my plans with Jack. The clock on the wall read just past 1am. Hopefully, I would be done and in bed, with Jack, by no later than 2:30am.

That was the plan anyway until Jack gently shook my shoulder. I had been working for no more than ten or fifteen minutes. The action startled me and I jumped, quickly removing my headset and whipping around only to remember that I was sharing my apartment tonight. At some point, Jack had changed into an over-sized shirt that looked like at some point it had belonged to Gideon. The white could barely be called that anymore and it was so thin it was almost see through. Across the front was a logo from some tech company and a date of the conference August 14-16, 2015. Jack's pierced nipples were visible and pressed against the thin fabric causing a flush to cross my cheeks. It was bizarre to see Jack like this. His make-up streaked across his face and pooled around his eye sockets. Probably from rubbing the sleep from them by the looks of the black marks on his hands. He looked like a cartoon depiction of a raccoon.

"Hey..." My greeting was cut off by Jack pouting at me. "Hey now, what's wrong?"

"Why aren't you in bed too?" He yawned. He seemed even smaller than usual, almost childlike in his questioning.

"Work." I gestured over my shoulder at the bright computer screen. "I'll be done shortly." Jack only pouted more. Without a word, he shuffled back into the bedroom seemingly accepting my answer. I chuckled and shook my head, returning to my work with a renewed sense of urgency.

It was around 2am when I finally finished. Cracking my knuckles as I waited for my computer to turn off, I looked over at my bedroom door. Light was visible from underneath. Had Jack been waiting for me and I didn't even noticed? I hoped not. I pushed the door open timidly, hoping to find Jack sound asleep and not angry that I had taken so long to finish my work. Once again, Jack was on the top of the covers having fallen back asleep while waiting for me. I shook my head and undressed, tucking Jack and myself into bed.

He was like a little space heater, so warm under my sheets. I had never truly shared a bed with someone else. Not like this anyway. A drunken hook-up or two, but nothing serious. Nothing even remotely resembling a longtime relationship. A lifetime of nights like this. Jack curled up against my chest, his soft breaths matching the rhythm of my own. I could get used to this.

VIII.

Dinners. Movies. Parks. Camping. We did everything we could fit in. The days were split between my work schedule and anything we could do to keep Jack out of his house. The weekends were entirely ours. Normally when Gideon was away Jack would just stay home and wait. Now Jack had the freedom to do anything he wanted. And he took advantage of that fact. There were days while I was at work Jack would stay at the mansion as well as some nights, as to not draw too much suspicion for why he was suddenly never home. The neighbors were full of gossip and he knew they would say something to Gideon. It also allowed him to check-in with Gideon through emails and the occasional video call at weird hours.

Days went by too quickly while we were together. The hours at work went by painfully slow. A month was not enough time, no matter what we did. In order to maximize our time together I even used the little bit of time off from work I had saved.

It was the happiest I had seen Jack. It took

some time for him to ease his nerves. There was always a looming threat Gideon would return early, or call and state that he knew what Jack was planning. After a week of nothing, he eased up. He kept his hair down, he smiled more, he actually seemed alive. Those big brown eyes sparkled in the light and in the darkness of the bedroom. Somehow, he grew more gorgeous as he gained a love of life with his newfound freedom. It was honestly the best month of my life too.

My work faltered, but I didn't care. I missed deadlines to take Jack out. Maxed out two credit cards on whatever and wherever Jack wanted. I wanted to show him everything that he was missing under Gideon. I had to. Jack deserved everything and so much more than I could give him. There would be time between when Gideon came back and we moved that I could use to make everything right again with my finances. I had no choice if we wanted to afford the move and start a life together. But until then? Whatever he wanted.

During dinner near the end of the second week, Jack explained that the days and nights at his house were becoming more and more unbearable. He was counting the days until Gideon would return and he would have to go back to pretending, hopefully not for long if we planned right. His voice was pained as he spoke and he squeezed my hand until it hurt. That drive, and need, to leave a life behind was something I understood. I had been there too.

"Oh, look at that one!" Jack jammed a finger hard enough at the computer screen to cause the colors to ripple.

"Careful!" I barked, swatting at his hand and receiving a pout in response. "But, yes. I like that one too." It was a little community of two-story apartment complexes with a park in the middle of it. It was also across the country from Gideon. Somewhere where Gideon wouldn't be able to retaliate when Jack broke the news. Somewhere we could start a new life – together. It wasn't big, but I didn't make enough money to afford the life of luxury Jack was used to receiving. Not that he knew that fact quite yet. It stretched the budget, but I could make it work. *We* could make it work.

We had it all figured out too. Jack would go back to Gideon for a bit while the lawyer worked on gathering paperwork, evidence, whatever was needed for the restraining order and the divorce. I would be the point of contact during that time as to not alert Gideon. Once the restraining order went through, Jack would stay at my place until the divorce was finalized. Hopefully we would halfway across the country by then too. The lawyer would fax over anything that still needed to be signed.

Jack would be able to finally get a job; I would be able to easily find something new too. The place was pet-friendly, unlike this apartment, so we could get a cat and/or a dog. There would be grocery shopping trips and date nights. No one around to know either of our pasts. Pure bliss – an idyllic life for the two of us.

Smiling, I leaned over and kissed Jack on the cheek while he leaned over my shoulder. The only sound was the click of the mouse as Jack looked through the photos. His eyes were focused and mouth open. He seemed to really like the apartment. That immediate connection with somewhere you felt you could imagine your life and call home.

“It reminds me of here.” Jack said, pointing at how the kitchen connected to the living room.

“Do you like it here?” I asked.

“I wish we could stay here.” Jack sighed deeply. A melancholy statement. I reached back and wrapped my arms around him, pulling him closer despite the computer chair that kept us apart.

“Maybe that is enough looking for today. You want to order in?” I asked, bookmarking the apartment and turning off the computer. I could see

Jack reflected back to me in the dark screens. It seemed to elongate his features, pulling those already almost too big eyes even larger. It was almost comical and I smiled, slowly standing up. "We could do Lucy's Diner again?" The greasy diner food seemed to be Jack's favorite, especially the large Belgian waffles with bananas and confectioner's sugar. Jack had a sweet tooth that was betrayed by the fact he was missing a few of his molars. Casualties from childhood gone unsupervised. There was also the slightly too bright canine tooth that was fake due to a fight him and Gideon had when they first started dating. These facts were extracted one by one, much like those teeth. Festering stories that over time led to pain, but then relief once you were finally rid of them.

There had been long nights of sitting on the couch and just talking. Long meandering conversations that often turned to our pasts, but only in small parts. Our conversations did not linger there long and these pieces were taken bit by bit. There was talk about the usual things like our favorite movies, as well arguments over radio stations and the subsequent compromise station. The two-hour-long conversation about cooking eggs and an even longer one about breakfast for dinner. Jack spoke of all the scandals his neighbors were involved with. Being kept at home meant he had a lot of time to people-watch and eavesdrop, and he certainly seemed to have a talent for it. Turns out that those made for TV movies weren't always incorrect. There were swingers, drugs, and cheating all up and down that block. No murder though, at least not that Jack knew. Money doesn't bring happiness, it would seem.

Jack and I also both shared a reluctance to share the sensitive subjects. Jack confided in me the story of his scars; which ones were from accidents like climbing trees or crashing his bike, and which ones came from less humorous sources such as himself or Gideon. While I had already known about his back, he went into detail the horrific ordeals his family and the Church had put him through in the name of God back in Rivière-du-Loup, Québec. In turn, Jack learned about my family back in Georgia. He learned about my business failures and about how my parents risked their house for me. My mother's early demise due to cancer. My guilt about not moving back home to take care of her.

As the days ran on, conversations turned to the more mundane such as who needed to pick up what and where our next dates would be. We started planning for the future, for what would be our lives together. Jack seemed to focus on planning the move, making sure that we picked the perfect place and often went above budget. My focus was on reigning Jack back into reality. Moving was expensive and not simple. Jack was raised in families where everything was taken care of for him, including now with Gideon. He had never held down a job and there was a lot he still needed to learn about the world, I quickly found out.

Over dinner that night, between mouthfuls of waffles, eggs, bacon, and some tortilla soup, we talked about how we would decorate that apartment we were considering. Jack wanted to repaint the walls to a robin's egg blue. I wanted to just hang pictures and posters up. We bickered, Jack waving his fork at me to the point a piece of waffle went flying and landed squarely in my lap. I jokingly dared him to eat it off and he obliged, crawling under the table. Our dinner remained unfinished. Left out to go cold.

~~~~~~~~~~~~~~~~~~~~~~~~~~~

Three weeks down, with one to go. It was a kind of melancholy breakfast as I got ready for work, realizing that we would be counting down the days until Gideon came back again. The loud buzzing from my phone broke me out of my gloom. "Have a
~~~~~~~~~~~~~~~~~~~~~~~~~~~

gr8 day :) XoXoX" read the text from Jack. I smiled and then sighed, my happiness quickly dissipating. How long after Gideon came back would we have to wait to move, to finalize the divorce? Jack said he had been looking into lawyers while I was at work, even going as far as calling a few who of them and getting quotes. Gideon would pay for it all, of course. Jack had a clear-cut case of domestic abuse and Gideon had all the money anyway.

Jack wasn't allowed access to the accounts, taxes, anything. Jack was lucky he could open his own mail in what was supposed to be his own house. As far as Gideon knew, he controlled everything in Jack's life. Jack spoke of Gideon and his control with a casual ease now, as if it was all already in the past. An ex who was just an asshole as opposed to an abusive husband whose presence still loomed over every aspect of his life.

He was going to have to go back to that, but finally he had a way out. That thought comforted us and according to Jack, gave him strength for what was yet to come. I still worried. Gideon was an unknown factor, a loose cannon who could turn violent at any second. Another buzz. "Cant w8 2 see u" the second text read. We had plans to go to the aquarium and I had taken a half-day to ensure that we could beat the crowds.

- VIII. -

I finished my work that day in three hours, leaving one agonizing hour before leaving and picking up Jack from my – no, our – apartment. Never did I pick Jack up from his own house, one habit that started out of necessity and continued out of caution. I ended up leaving an extra half an hour early in order to make a pit stop. Jack and I had only one week left together before everything would be set in motion again. Right now, we were in a weird kind of stasis where we could be with each other, but still not entirely. I wanted to show him that this wasn't going to be over once Gideon came back. I wanted to show that I would be there through the divorce, no matter how rough it got.

A green emerald – Jack's birth stone – caught the light and glittered. Something simple, just a diamond-cut emerald on a white gold band. Gideon had all the money in the world, Gideon could get Jack anything he wanted and yet somehow didn't bother. Sure, there were things here and there, but always after a fight as a way to apologize for the black eyes, bruises, and broken teeth. Bile rose in my throat and I wondered if it was the same color as the emerald or as black as it tasted. I pocketed the ring, planning to give it to Jack before we left the aquarium that afternoon, before dinner. A small gift that hopefully would show how serious I was about all of this. A promise.

When I came home, running slightly late due to an accident, I found Jack rousing from a nap on the couch in one of my old ratty t-shirts. He rubbed his eyes, looking up to the cat clock that lazily swung above the TV.

"You're late." He grunted, throwing his legs over the top of the couch and sitting on the back of it to stare at me through half-lidded eyes. Every time he did this, my heart stopped as I waited for him to flip the couch. It never happened due to Jack's size, but it got me every time.

"Sorry, there was an accident." I called after Jack as he slunk off to the bathroom. "We have to leave in 30 minutes. Will that be enough time?" Jack took an ungodly amount of time to get ready, often doing and redoing his hair and make-up several times. I had to fight back my annoyance at the fact he hadn't even started his routine yet. He did this every time and yet, it still got to me.

"Better hope it is." Jack called from the bathroom, the now familiar noises of Jack's make-up clattering on the bathroom counter. My groaned response went unheard. I followed after him and he idly chatted about my work day as he got ready. Watching him do his make-up, wipe it off, and try again was always something of a show for me. I always thought it looked fine, but Jack never agreed.

Too thick or uneven that time, not enough another. Even his hair which would never stay up was a process. As the minutes ticked by and I began to get antsy, I swore Jack went slower.

Luckily, it was just enough time. Almost. We arrived to the aquarium five minutes later than our tickets were for. Jack was frantic, pulling me both excitedly and nervously to the door. He acted as if we were the first people to ever be late. The desk clerk didn't even check the times as they scanned the tickets, too busy looking at the group of third graders who were noisily clambering off a bus behind us. A never-ending parade that grew in volume as the group grew in size. Jack and I hurried inside, hoping to beat the sea of children who would likely destroy any peace.

Jack pressed his face to every glass he could trying to see every fish in every enclosure. He eagerly read each information panel and took photos with his phone. He was not unlike the most enthusiastic third graders who caught up to us and at one point sharing an animated conversation with a young girl about clown fish and *Finding Nemo*. After that, the third graders bypassed us, skipping a lot of the more complex exhibits such as the shark walk. I don't think Jack really wanted to walk over the hot, humid salt water tank, but he did it anyway for the sake of doing everything.

"Can we stay to watch the penguin feeding?" Jack pleaded while hanging off my arm. According to the sign, we had arrived about an hour and a half early. Looking at the map, we only had maybe about twenty minutes left of things to see. Forty to an hour if we continued at Jack's pace.

"Jack, I don't-" The puppy dog eyes. Always with the puppy dog eyes. I groaned and shook my head. "Fine. Fine." I conceded and laughed, pulling Jack in for a hug. I could find something to do on my phone if I somehow grew tired of watching Jack flit between exhibits like a hummingbird with just as much energy.

"Oh! Let's go pet the stingrays!" Jack began pulling me in the direction of the fancy kiddy pool where visitors could annoy the animals. Jack's eyes were practically sparkling with excitement. The area was created to look like a mock beach, the little pool raised up enough to not be too high for anyone old enough to touch the lazily swimming creatures. I watched as they glided through the water playfully dodging around some guests' fingers while splashing others. At least they seemed to be enjoying the attention.

"It splashed me!" Jack whined, sounding offended that the stingray had splashed some of the mock-ocean water on him.

"It happens. Just pet it." I dipped my fingers into the water, gently pressing against the spongy yet somewhat soft fin, flap, or whatever it was. Same as the instructor was showing to everyone who walked up to the pool. They felt like a pool noodle mixed with wet velvet. Out of the corner of my eye I watched Jack.

He gripped the edges of the tank to until the veins in his hands were bulging and strained. His eyes became distant as he watched the rays swim around their enclosure. Every time there was a splashing noise Jack's eyes darted to the offending ray. There was an awe in that gaze, a dreamy quality, as he watched the rays glide in slow circles. They showed personality and Jack's eyes moved from each one as they reacted to each visitor. He was absolutely enthralled by them.

"They look like angels." The words were almost a whisper as Jack reached his hand into the water. His lip curled as the warm water touched his skin. The salt probably burned his chewed husks that he called fingernails. A habit that got worse as the month began to come to an end. One of the rays swam up but dived quickly out of Jack's reach. That curled lip turned into a pout. How adorable he looked as he stood there, trying to reach the rays just out of touch. I pulled my phone from my pocket, wanting to take a few candid shots. Jack looked... happy. Sure, he wasn't smiling, but his body was relaxed. He was focused on something happening, not gazing into the distance. He was present. Everything was normal.

The fingers on my free hand played with the ring in my pocket. This would be a perfect time to give it to Jack. The perfect moment to show and tell Jack how serious I was about everything. Our future. Our plans. I squeezed it in my palm, feeling the stone bite into my flesh as I tried to steel my queasy stomach. Jack had no idea that it was coming and he would be absolutely floored. Not a proposal, but it would definitely look like one minus me dropping to one knee. Maybe I-

A loud splash broke the moment caused by Jack violently yanking his hand back. My phone fumbled in my hand, but I caught it before it almost comically tumbled into the water. The stingrays didn't seem bothered by the sudden movement as they were probably used to children coming up and splashing all day. They continued to lazily swim in circles, their habit unbroken. Jack on the other hand was walking away, cradling his hand like it had been bitten.

"Where are you going?" I called after him. I

moved through the families that Jack could somehow navigate. He slipped through them like a trained assassin or thief, his slight frame making it easier. He didn't acknowledge me and continued on. I started to lose him, occasionally calling his name. People were staring. My skin was crawling with their gaze but I didn't care. I needed to get to Jack. I had to find out what happened. Did he get bit by one despite what the instructor said? Was he trying to find somewhere to pout about how they didn't like him? The idea brought a small smile to my face. And yet, there was a sick feeling pulling at my insides.

When I finally caught up to him he stood in the middle of one of the large round entrance rooms that connected the whole building. Each offshoot led to a different section of the aquarium with a surrounding ring with the center being where we were. Light from the ceiling illuminated him and people moved around him, casting suspicious sideways glances. Couples hurried past and parents pushed their children by with hushed whispers. I grabbed his arm and spun him around, panting. His eyes were distant and wide, staring through me. I knew that look.

"Judah," he whispered. "Judah, he's here." Jack's fingers dug into my shoulders. Really digging into me until it hurt. His hands were still damp from the stingray pool.

"Who?" The words slipped out before I realized what Jack was saying.

The fear in Jack's eyes, no, the absolute terror reflected in his pale face confirmed everything I needed to know. Gideon was here. I feel simultaneously heavy and like I was about to drift away. Every nerve in my body turned to ice. The queasiness from earlier returned, but with an acrid taste at the back of my throat.

We had been so careful. Jack had checked in frequently with Gideon through email and the occasional video call. Jack checked his itinerary every day too, just in case Gideon decided to come back early and surprise him. We had been so careful. So fucking careful. And yet, apparently, here he was. Gideon fucking Bellview. A whole week early. Surprise, surprise. This meant only one thing, one awful thing. Gideon knew.

IX.

Time slowed to a crawl as Gideon walked over to Jack and I. His massive hands were shoved into his pockets, but you could see the bulge of his fists against his black dress pants. Each step in those impeccable dress shoes clicked on the aquarium tile and echoed into infinity in my head. Reality came crashing down in loud, glass-shattering waves. Gideon was here. He knew. How?

"Judah." Gideon stood in front of me, looking down. His size blocked out the sun coming down from the skylight above, dimming it and bringing the weight of his oppressive shadow. "What a coincidence to see you two here." Gideon smiled. There was no friendliness or warmth in that smile. I half expected a snake's forked tongue to flick out between his teeth. "I thought you were out doing some shopping, Jack." His tone remained even and without emotion as he turned towards his husband. Every word said deliberately and drawn out like a parent catching a toddler in a lie. The exact same way he had spoken to Jack the night I had met him at the bar.

"I-I-..." Jack stammered, eyes locked with Gideon. His body trembled and he withdrew, moving to step behind me and then thinking better of it. His breathing came in rapid bursts and his eyes wide. He looked like a mouse cornered by a snake in a terrarium. Those big dark eyes filled with an all-knowing fear of what comes next. Nowhere to go. Nowhere to hide.

"Not here, Gideon. It's not what you think." I kept my tone flat yet commanding. Gideon couldn't know the way my guts were twisting up inside due to how terrified I was. I couldn't let him think he was in control of the situation.

"Please, like the first time you fucked I didn't know." Gideon snarled. His lips curled and he flashed his teeth. "I'm not an idiot. I've known, for awhile now." Venom on every word. He broke eye contact with Jack and turned that piercing gaze back to me. How could he have known, especially on that night? My confusion must have been spread across my face as he laughed, a deep echoing sound that made my head hurt.

"You really think I would just drop Jack off?" His grin looked predatory gleaming in the light. "I was in the parking lot across the street. I watched you pick him up."

"But..." I had no answer to this. How could we

have been so stupid? So foolish? How did that not cross our minds? How did Jack not notice Gideon's car? The world began to spin, lights gaining all too bright halos.

"Let's take this outside. Please. Not here. Gideon, Sweety, please." Words tumbled and spilled from Jack's lips. His trembling fingers grabbed onto the cuff of Gideon's shirt. When had he moved to over there? Gideon snarled, violently ripping his sleeve from Jack's grasp. Fire danced in Gideon's eyes as he inspected the damage to his shirt. Jack took two steps back and looked around him. The aquarium was starting to empty out at this point. Both school children and couples alike had left. Those who remained were quickly shuffling into other parts of the building. Parents pushed children by, grabbing them by their arms and dragging them if they had to. No employees were visible either. In a matter of moments, only the three of us stood in that center hall.

"You...you're home early." Jack stammered. What was he trying to do? Was he not paying attention to what his husband was saying?

Gideon held up his hand and Jack bit his lip to silence himself. "Please. I'll talk to you later about you and your schemes." Gideon said coldly. Acid bubbled in the back of my throat, burning in my nostrils.

"Then why now? Huh?" I spat, unable to hide my anger. I could feel the fire in my chest, threatening to burn its way up just as the acid already was. My hands were going numb. I stepped forward, clenching and unclenching my fists. My shirt suddenly felt too tight and my breathing too heavy and loud. Gideon eyed me, not sizing me up but with contempt. My skin crawled. "Why make a public spectacle?" I asked, hoping to keep some control over the situation.

"He was planning on trying to leave." Gideon snarled. "This charade has gone on long enough. I figured it was time to end it early. Before it got too serious." Gideon even hissed the word serious.

Despite being on a few inches off of Gideon, I felt so small standing in that empty room before him. He towered over me with his heavy brows furrowed in white hot anger. "It was cute at first, Jack thinking he could play house with someone else for a bit, but this is over now." Gideon's demeanor was stern and controlled. Under the surface, I could see the anger threatening to bubble over at any second – a hair trigger waiting for a reason to be pulled.

"And not to mention, Judah," the way he said my name made me want to vomit. "A married man, really?" Gideon snorted and shook his head. "How low can you go?" He clicked his tongue against his teeth to scold me. He looked back at Jack, who was slowly backing away, trying to use this confrontation as a means to escape. "And you," Gideon continued, causing Jack to freeze in place. "Imagine what your family would say about a divorce! And adultery to boot!" Gideon laughed. A sound that was so full of itself. So sure it had said the most harmful thing possible.

"You really think Jack cares about what his family thinks?" My nostrils flared as my nails dug into the palms of my hands. Gideon knew nothing about Jack despite their long history. He really did think of him as just an object to be dragged and tossed around as he willed.

"Of course! Imagine the papers, the stories about what a little whore-"

Seeing red is literal sometimes. Hitting someone in the face hurts. The dull sound of flesh on flesh rang through the room, causing Jack to gasp in surprise. Getting hit in the face by an ex-college football player hurts more. Apparently being more than a few years removed didn't change that fact. Gideon's fist connected and the crunch that followed was either Gideon's hand or my cheekbone. My glasses were knocked from my face and skittered across the floor.

The next several minutes were a blur of fists, both of us wrestling each other to the ground and hitting where ever we could. Chest, face, back, a hit even connected with my hip letting me know that Gideon was probably aiming for my junk. While previous sounds had seem to echo, the dull thuds of our fists and our grunts of pain and frustration seemed to exist in a vacuum. They rang hollow and empty, either due to my focus on the fight or the several punches to my head and face. The only thing that seemed to break free was the sharp sound of clothing ripping. And Jack's screaming.

Jack was begging for us to stop. Pleading and crying for us to stop. For Gideon to just talk to him outside. I could see him out of the corner of my swelling eye, hands clasped over his mouth. Meticulously done make-up began to smear and run in a way I hadn't seen in awhile. My heart sank long enough for Gideon to get another hit to my face with my nose crunching underneath.

Security pulled us apart, still swinging and growling. We were two feral cavemen with only blood on the mind. Blood that was pouring down my cheek and mouth. A coppery taste that made me spit without thinking. Gideon's eye was beginning to swell, giving some definition to his flat face. Our chests and shoulders heaved and Gideon wheezed letting me know I got a few good shots in to match my bleeding face. Or his age was showing. I like to think that I had got a few good hits in.

"You all need to leave. Now. The police are on their way." The security guards, who looked like they hadn't had anything to do in their years at the aquarium, were breathing just as hard as we were. The one who spoke had his hands up in attempt to show he was peaceful. Gideon and I were at least half a foot taller and even Gideon was probably a good decade or two younger. Either one of us could easily take him if we wanted to. There was no way he could take either of us in a fight and he knew it.

"Fuck you." I spit again at Gideon and turned to leave, offering my hand to Jack. "Fuck him. Let's go." My voice still hard as I spoke to the trembling mess that Jack had become.

Jack's brown eyes turned from me and to Gideon. "I..." He whimpered, chewing over his lip until it was stained red with blood to match mine. "I..." He shifted his weight, rubbing his arms roughly, eyes rapidly darting between Gideon and I.

"Jack. Come." Gideon called him like a dog. After wiping blood from his face onto his torn sleeve, Gideon waved him over. Jack locked eyes with me and they said everything I needed to know as he walked over to Gideon. In order to leave, they had to walk past me, with Jack clutching tightly to Gideon's arm. Before they left through a fire exit, held open by the guard, Jack turned his head and mouthed to me. "I'm sorry."

I was still there when the cops showed up. I gave my statement. No, I wasn't pressing charges. Yes, I started the fight. I even gave them Gideon's address so they could get a statement from him as well. While I was talking to the police, the security guard found a towel from somewhere to wipe my face with. As the cops left and I went to leave with them, the security guard took my dirty towel and shook his head.

"I hope she's worth it." He handed me my glasses and walked away without another word.

Returning to my car without Jack felt wrong. Everything felt wrong. I banged my bruised hands on the steering wheel while shouting any expletive I could think of to call Gideon. He had ruined everything. We had been so close, so goddamned close, and he swooped in and ruined it all because he could. Gideon had felt threatened, meaning that it was real. So real and so close that Gideon truly felt he was going to lose Jack.

Tears dotted my steering wheel and I wiped my nose on my sleeve, leaving a disgusting trail of snot and blood that would absolutely stain my favorite band shirt. What an idiot, I thought to myself before sniffling and tasting the bitter combination in the back of my throat. I could feel the ring biting into my ass as I shifted in my seat. The ring...

I removed it from my back pocket, letting it fall around my middle finger. It was way too small, not making it past my first knuckle. The stone caught the fading sun, shooting green tinted brilliance across the inside of my car. The way it glimmered in the dimming light made me sigh and think of Jack immediately before the fight. Immediately before our world had come crashing down. So happy, so peaceful and content. How Jack should be. Not that shaking and fearful mess he became the moment he saw Gideon.

Anger ripped through me and I threw the ring, hearing it ping off my windshield before disappearing in the trash under the passenger seat. A mix of empty coffee cups (something Jack demanded every morning), fast food bags, a condom wrapper or two (Jack was...adventurous to say the least), and Lord knows what else Jack had thrown down there. Memories of our happy and undisturbed moments together.

“I’ll find it later...” I mumbled to no one

before reluctantly leaving the parking lot. Back to my empty apartment full of Jack's things, left there unwillingly and for an unknown amount of time now. An endless sea of reminders of what should have been.

After the fight, Jack texted me once to tell me to leave him alone. I tried to call but, the number was disconnected already. No matter how many time I tried I only got through to a robot telling me that the number was no longer in service. I returned to wait at Helena's, but everything had changed there too. In the month we had ignored the bar for our own private activities, everyone seemed to grow cold. No longer did the bartender even try to serve me drinks as I spent the long, lonely hours there. This also meant I wasn't scolded for bringing my own drinks to pass the time. I drove myself home more times than I probably should have.

Long lonely nights with no one to talk to. The bartender wouldn't even try to make small talk with me and I tried. I tried and tried. Just the bottle to drown my sorrows in. Work wasn't much help either. Hangovers are hard to work through and even when those stopped, there was no motivation there. What was the point to anything?

I would drive by Jack's house to make sure he was still alive. The times I did see him, he was sitting on the porch, working in the garden, or silhouetted behind one of the many curtained windows. Every time my heart would slam into my throat. What if Gideon was home? What if someone started to recognize me or my car? Gideon was never there and I never dared to do more than drive by and pray Jack knew I was watching somehow.

On days I couldn't see Jack, I parked my car outside. Never for long, at first at least. The driveway was empty, Gideon would be at work, so what was the danger? Even the video doorbell wouldn't be able to pick me up from across the street, right? I would wait for about ten to thirty minutes before driving away, some days never getting a glimpse of Jack. Those days were the longest and the hardest. No confirmation to stop my mind from racing through the most awful possibilities.

Not this day though. I had just put my car in park when Jack walked outside. By the looks of the tools in his hand, the large, dark sunglasses and the comically large wide-brimmed hat on his head, he was about to work on the garden. A garden that was already weed free, methodically organized, and eerily perfect. Hedges not only elegantly trimmed, but also full of intricate designs that needed more upkeep than the garden did. The whole mansion looked like something out of a home and garden magazine. Jack stood out in dark contrast against the red door. A neighbor called from two doors down and Jack waved, shyly. He walked down the steps, watching each step as if it would suddenly fall out from under him. In his concentration he didn't even notice the tools tumbling from his arms.

Instinctively, I opened my car door and went to step out. I had one leg out the door before I realized what I was doing. I got back into my car and shut the door. The noise caused Jack's head to snap up and he saw me. Even with the sunglasses I knew our eyes were locked. An eternity passed as we stared at each other. A car drove by and the last thing I saw was that red door slamming shut, the gardening tools still left scattered on the porch stairs.

When I got home I tried Jack's cellphone again.

"The number you have dialed is no longer in service." The robot woman on the other end answered before disconnecting. Then my phone rang before I could even put it down.

"Jack!?" I answered without checking the caller ID.

"Judah. It's Alex." My heart sank. My boss.

"Oh, hey Alex." I said, sinking into my couch.

"Listen, Judah, we need to talk." That condescending tone. A tone I had gotten used to in my life lately. "Your work lately," she continued, "it's been less than...satisfactory." She held that last word out for emphasis, making sure that I knew I was in trouble.

"Yeah, yeah, I know. I'm sorry, Alex. I just have some stuff going on and-"

"Sure, sure." She interjected. "But, unfortunately, it's caused too many delays. We're already a week off from launch and have at least two weeks of work still to do."

"I get it. I really do. I'll crunch. Just, give me another day." I pleaded. I couldn't lose my job now too. Not after everything.

"Judah." Did she really need to say my name so much? "I know about the fight. That man showed up here looking for you that day too." She sounded scared for a moment. "And now this? It's too much." Had Gideon threatened her? My skin crawled with the violation.

"Alex, please. Just-"

"No, Judah. No more excuses. You're fired." Alex hung up the phone.

- X. -

Not only had Gideon ruined Jack and I's plans, he ruined my work life too. I had lost Jack and my job. My apartment would be next and where would I go then? Georgia wasn't an option. The plan had been the only option. It remained the only option. But how? Tears rolled down my cheeks and my head hung heavy. I cried until my throat hurt. I cried until my eyes hurt. I cried until the snot dripped from my chin and onto my phone. I cried until I needed a drink. A strong one.

Helena's looked strange lit up by the light of day. With no shadows to hide the fading exterior, the bar seemed even more run down than I had previously thought. The siding was faded in some places and brightly patched in others, creating a weird patchwork contrast against the pitch black door. Even the parking lot was filled with more weeds than I had noticed before. If I didn't know better, I would have believed Helena's had been abandoned for months. At least the sign looked more complete in the day. You couldn't tell that most of the letters were no longer working. The bartender was still unlocking and unpacking when I walked in. He took one look at me and looked away before talking to the young woman behind the counter. She took a quick glance at me and I waved. She disappeared into the back. I sat down in the second to last seat before tapping my knuckles on the bar. My apartment was dry and I really needed a drink.

"Hey, can I-"

"No." The bartender responded curtly before disappearing into the back as well. I hopped behind the bar, poured myself a double, and left a $20 on the register. The drink was already half gone by the time the bartender and his trainee came back out with several new bottles. Confusion filled the bartender's face as he saw the money but then saw the quickly emptying drink before me. He groaned and just dropped the bottle in front of me before moving to restock. Mission accomplished.

With my last bit of cash gone, I switched to my debit card. And as long as it was swiping, I was drinking. The bottle had been drained a long time before and the bartender eyed me after every drink, wondering when to cut me off. Somehow, none of it seemed to matter. Guess whatever issue he had about giving me drinks before was over now. Money was money and from the looks of the outside, it was sorely needed. After what felt like the twentieth bathroom trip, the room wasn't even beginning to spin. Was I paying for water? I snorted and took another drink, feeling the burn and confirming. Definitely not water.

Every time that door opened I would feel my

heart leap into my throat, feeling a sudden rush hoping it was Jack. Each time it wasn't and my heart dropped, I could feel the liquor sloshing around in my stomach like a stone dropped into Lush Lake.

My glass was empty and the world was finally swimming, just how I needed it. At first, I didn't think he was real. Jack said nothing as he walked over to me, grabbing my keys out of my pocket, and left. He was wearing those giant reflective sunglasses which only meant one thing. In my drunken stupor, it took me a moment to realize who it was. I almost punched him, but he was halfway across the bar before I could even turn around. I followed wordlessly behind him – chasing a ghost.

"Jack?" He was nowhere to be found when I stumbled outside. Looking around, there was no sign he was even there until I noticed the lights on in my car. I definitely hadn't left them this whole time. The night was cold, way too cold for April. With no jacket, I shivered and rubbed my arms. The temperature sobered me as I walked across the parking lot. Curled up on my passenger seat lay Jack with his forehead pressed against the cool window. I opened the driver's side door and slid in. My keys dangled weakly in Jack's already outstretched hand.

"Jack, I..." I wasn't even sure what I was going to say. I'm sorry? I'm happy to see you? I'm an idiot? I almost got you killed? I don't know. The hurt, strangled whimper from Jack told me everything I needed to know. Not now. The engine turned and we drove to my place with the only sound being Jack's heavy breathing.

"I'm leaving him." The words spilled out of Jack the moment he heard the door shut to the apartment. "I'm leaving him, Judah." Jack stepped into my arms, face buried in my chest.

"I'm leaving him." Jack repeated. That's when I realized that he wasn't telling me. He was convincing himself. Silently, I held him close. I didn't speak. I didn't know what to say. What could I say?

Jack swallowed hard. He bit his lip and air hissed past his teeth with a whistle. One of his teeth was broken. On his hand was a bright new ring. Even his earrings, dangling gold geometry, looked new. He removed his sunglasses and for the first time, I saw the true extent of Gideon's damage. His eyes were red from burst blood vessels, their cause a bruise fading to a sickly green around his throat. Around his neck was a strip of black fabric, a pathetic attempt to hide the marks of Gideon's abuse. This was the first time I had seen Jack outside without make-up too, which caused the bruises and cuts to stand out in bright contrast against his sickly pale skin.

He moved quietly to the bedroom, the bed creaking under his weight. His face was in his hands when I came into the bedroom. As I sat next to him, he recoiled for a moment before pressing himself into me. He was shaking.

"I can't get it out of my mouth. I can't get it out of my mouth." He swallowed hard again. Like it was difficult. Like it hurt. "Judah... It's all I can taste." I turned pulling Jack into my lap. I didn't know what to say. I didn't know what to do. So, I let Jack explain what had happened in those weeks.

"When we came home, he didn't say anything. He wouldn't speak to me. He wouldn't look at me." Jack started to shake harder, pressing himself harder into me. "I...I...told him I was sorry. That I was just wrong and stupid. I told him what I thought he wanted to hear." Jack clicked his tongue. "And...and he said 'ok'. He went back to the Gideon I knew before. Back in the beginning, before we were married. We went out together. We went shopping. He listened to me. He...he seemed to finally understand what I needed." Jack pulled away, wringing his hands in his lap. "It all went back to normal." His breath whistled in and out of his parted lips.

"You...were going to stay?" My words didn't

hide my hurt. After everything he had risked, he was going to stay with Gideon? After all our plans? I lost everything and he was going to ignore that? Just up and ignore everything I had done for him in that month together and stay with Gideon?

"I...I'm sorry Judah. I...I don't know what to say. I've been with Gideon forever! I...I couldn't just throw it away!" Those bloodshot eyes stared at me – terrified. "He's given me everything I have." He chewed on his lip, pulling a scab off and causing it to bleed. His hand raised to his lip, and he tried to wipe away the blood but managed to only smear it across his face.

I opened my mouth to say something, but then shut it. Jack needed to know he was wrong. Gideon had given him nothing. Everything Gideon did was an empty gesture to maintain control. I stared into Jack's eyes, taking in the bruises around his neck and the cuts on his face. There was the broken tooth and across his temple was a hastily glued together gash. My fingers reached out, letting my thumb gently run across the jagged scab. Jack had to know that he deserved better. He didn't need me to try and convince him otherwise. Not right now.

"But...whenever I tried to go out by myself, he would lose it. First, he was suspicious I was visiting you. He would follow me, even when I just went to go out to the garden." Jack started to sob. "Then, every little thing turned into how I was cheating on him. He constantly hung it over me whenever I did anything wrong..."

"He showed me the photos. Of us together. He got more and more violent after that." Jack continued. Slender fingers gently touched the bruise around his neck. While Jack had always been a nervous nail biter, every single one was bitten until it was red and angry. There was blood under what remained of his fingernails. His whole body shook and he gagged, running to the bathroom. The dry heaving could be heard from down the hall. Then silence.

I was in shock. Gideon really knew that Jack and I were having an affair from the beginning? He had photos of us having said affair. That would explain how he found us at the aquarium. How he seemed to just be watching from a distance. He wanted to see with his own eyes what he already knew. More concrete proof than what he already had. Put aside every doubt as to what was going on between Jack and I.

Gideon had been truly watching the whole time. My brain flashed back through every meeting and interaction with Jack, both in and outside of

Helena's. I thought of that car that drove by so slowly the night of Jack and I's fight. Was that Gideon, checking in to see what his husband was really up to? Was Gideon watching now? Goose bumps crept up my arms at the thought of being watched in my own apartment. How? Where?

Jack shuffled back and laid down. More like deflated onto the bed. He curled up tightly against my back, trying to disappear into himself it looked like. And yet he continued on.

"I went out to get the mail once and ended up talking to the neighbor...I was gone too long." Jack sighed heavily. "I was hoping I would see you again. Like I had earlier. Gideon got mad. We got into a fight. I told him that I was going to leave..." Jack's voice became monotone. There was no emotion to the words he spoke next.

"He beat me with his gun. He broke my tooth while he shoved it into my mouth and told me if I ever tried to set foot outside of the house again that it would be in a body bag. That he would *personally* see to it." Jack fell silent after that. His breathing was hot and jagged against my back as my shirt became wet. "So I ran to the only place I could." To me.

We sat in that silence for awhile. The weight of the air was heavy. Every breath seemed to be a fight. It was like sucking in the hot and humid air during the worst parts of the Georgia summer. At some point, we fell asleep in each other's arms. Not another word was spoken between us about that night or that incident. The next time I woke up, Jack was gone.

"The number you have dialed is no longer in service. Please hang up and-" I hung up before the robot attendant could finish the same speech I had heard every time I had tried calling since the aquarium. Was this part of whatever new plan Jack had hinted at? How long was I to wait for step two? For further instructions? The previous night hung heavy in my mind, along with his sudden disappearance – a hungry and vacuous void. What had happened during the night? Did Gideon come calling? Did Jack decide to go into hiding? Did he leave without me? That last thought cut through me. Jack said he was leaving but, he didn't say I was coming with him. He didn't say he was leaving with me specifically. Was last night a goodbye and I didn't even know it? So many questions left without answers.

Driving by Jack's house did not give me any answers either. The driveway remained empty, the lights off and blinds drawn. It looked unoccupied and as hollow as I felt. A shiver ran through me. Weeds had began to sprout in Jack's normally meticulous garden. No warmth seemed to radiate from this place as it had done before, in spite of the events that took place inside. That feeling disturbed me. It set my teeth on edge. Everything felt increasingly wrong.

I waited the night at Helena's. The bartender and his new employee spent most of the night talking and sending sidelong glances down my way as I waited for Jack to show up. I drove by the house again on my way home and still nothing. Not even the porch light was on and the driveway remained empty. Where had they gone? Did Gideon kidnap Jack? Or something more sinister? I shook my head and took a deep breath, white knuckling the steering wheel as I crept by. Don't go there Judah, I thought to myself.

The thought to call the cops come across my mind. Then I thought better of it. One day didn't mean anything, especially with Gideon somewhat frequently going out on business trips. Plus, the cops wouldn't do anything more than give me weird looks, take my statement (if that) and that would be the end of the investigation. Jack could have been staying somewhere else, maybe a neighbor's? Somewhere that Gideon wouldn't come looking for him? Maybe that's where Gideon was – out looking for Jack. I hoped and for the first time in a long time, I prayed.

After a few days, Gideon's car returned. Yet, I still did not see Jack. I spent minutes and then hours outside of that mansion. I grew accustomed to every cracked brick and crooked porch stair. The more I stared at the house, the more sinister it became, seeming to decay and fall into disrepair before my eyes even though I knew that wasn't true. I saw Gideon's large silhouette occasionally upstairs, but never did I see anything that suggested Jack was there.

Where was he hiding? Did he truly already leave without me? These thoughts spun through my mind as I was coming home from work. My hours spent outside the mansion had been fruitless. That morning I didn't see Gideon or Jack and Alex had asked me to come and clear my desk. It wasn't much, just my own equipment and a few fidget toys for the slower days. Not even a full box's worth.

When I saw Gideon standing in front of my apartment, anger flared inside of me. What did he want? His black suit looked like it cost more than I used to make in a month and honestly, probably did. Despite the heavy clouds in the sky, he had dark shades over his eyes. He looked like a shitty celebrity bodyguard instead of one of the richest men in the city. I sneered at the idea as I stepped out of my car.

“The fuck do you want!?” I slammed the door shut. Gideon crossed his arms. His mouth was pulled tight at the corners. He looked uncomfortable, like he didn’t want to be here either. How long had he been waiting for me?

“I need to speak to you.” Gideon spoke in that same flat voice devoid of emotion. It made my blood boil.

“What did you do with Jack? Where is he?” I yelled.

“Jack’s dead.” Gideon said it so matter of fact. He raised his sunglasses up and rested them on the top of his head. The world swam. I leaned against my car before taking a deep breath as my legs started to give way. He’s just fucking with you. Jack is leaving him so he’s trying to keep him imprisoned or something. This was just a ruse. I glared at Gideon, unable to catch my breath or find the words to speak. Those eyes bore into me and he repeated it again, as if he thought I didn’t hear him. “Jack’s dead, Judah.”

Gideon continued. “He killed himself last night. I came home from work and he was on the bathroom floor.” Gideon set his jaw and shifted his weight. “He took my gun and shot himself.” The words seemed to visibly hurt Gideon. His knuckles became as he grabbed his forearms and the color drained from his face as well. He shifted his weight between his feet, unable to find a way to stand. Tears seemed to be pooling in his deep set eyes, unable to be hidden by his heavy brows. Suddenly I realized Gideon looked like he hadn't slept in days.

My legs fully gave out and I slid to sit against my car. My fingers tangled in my hair, pulling on it in large fistfuls. This wasn't some sick version of a joke from Gideon. What he said was the truth. That haunted looked on his face confirmed it all.

Jack was dead.

Gideon went to leave without saying anything more, climbing into his luxury sports car with the tinted windows which stood out against the economy sedans that filled the parking lot. He pulled up next to me, eyes staring straight ahead and not even bothering to look towards me.

"The funeral is in a week. Don't make a scene." Then he left, peeling out of the parking lot with a screech that only shattered my thoughts more. Leaning against my car, I sat there until one of my neighbor's pulled in. They asked if I was alright, but everything sounded underwater. I must have looked at them and answered because they walked into their apartment shortly after. I remained outside until the sun started to set. I don't remember making it into my apartment or to my bed, but I must have at some point.

I woke up in the middle of the night to a cold sweat. Events earlier in the day seemed to be a haze, a bad dream – or more like the worst nightmare. I felt sick. Was there a chance that I had really dreamed Jack was dead? I tried his cellphone and was greeted by that robotic voice once more. That didn't prove anything though, his phone had been off since that night at the aquarium.

I didn't bother changing since I was still in my clothes from earlier. I slid my shoes on and floated down and out of the apartment and to my car. Did I really want to do this? What good would confirming Jack was dead do? Inhaling deeply, I opened the door and got in, mentally preparing myself as best I could to drive by the mansion.

Yellow police tape was on the door. Despite the time of night, there were still police there working the scene. Gideon's car was nowhere in site as I drove by. Every light was on in the house, illuminating it like a spotlight compared to the other houses whose lights were all off. I looked at my clock, and it wasn't even past 11pm yet. Jack had been dead for several hours now according to Gideon. Yet, he had the funeral already planned? My mind was blank as I drove home, except for something tugging at the corners of it just out of reach. There was just something that didn't sit right with me...

~~~~~~~~~~~~~~~~~~~~~~~~~~~~

The next week was a blur. I don't know how I made it through the days. There were so many questions that wouldn't ever have answers. Did he really kill himself? The thought soured in my stomach and I gritted my teeth. That means Jack had been home those days I drove by. Right? Where else would he have been if I never saw him behind those curtains, outside, or at Helena's? The plan was to finally get out of there and start living how he had hoped life would be. Then to go and kill himself? It didn't seem right. None of this seemed right.

There was another explanation that made more sense to me. Jack was leaving and so Gideon decided to kill him. Gideon had threatened him only the week before with murder. Not only threatened him, but had beaten him with the very gun that would be the object of his demise. Shooting himself with Gideon's gun was a pretty convenient story. Coming home from work to Jack dead was a real
~~~~~~~~~~~~~~~~~~~~~~~~~~~~

damn easy story to swallow with Jack's past. Gideon had an easy alibi, and he knew it.

Someone surely had to have heard the gunshot, right? And with Gideon's past abusive behavior, there had to be at least one or two domestic dispute calls to their residence. Surely there would be some sort of public record that could be found that would prove that Jack didn't kill himself. Something off about the timing of the shot, the 911 call, anything. I could potentially talk to the lawyer Jack had been speaking to before Gideon came back.

Gideon had to have killed him. It was easier and more convenient than trying to hide a body anyway. People would ask questions if Gideon's husband suddenly up and disappeared. Plus, there would be the public speculation and ridicule that would come with a missing husband. But, suicide? Nice and tidy. No loose ends to worry about.

These thoughts stormed in my head as I pulled up to the church. Not many cars were in the parking lot and I recognized most of them, including Gideon's. Jack was well liked by everyone he met, but Gideon kept him on a short leash, so it was mostly the neighbors and maybe a few connections through Gideon. Less people to question Jack's sudden death as well. The taste of blood filled my mouth as I had been chewing on my lip out of anger. Now was not the time or place for these emotions, I thought as I pulled into the spot next to Gideon's. "Don't make a scene" echoed in my head.

Despite the occasion the sun was bright and it was humid for the season, almost oppressively so. Jack would have loved to spend a day like this in a park. Despite the dark clothes he normally wore, the heat never seemed to bother him like it did everyone else. The thought brought a smile to my face before reality brought me back to where we were and why. The church Gideon had picked was a Catholic one – the oldest in the area. I was slightly surprised to see such a large and well-known establishment holding the funeral services for a queer man who had supposedly committed suicide. Money goes a long way, and the church was no exception. Respect for Jack's life and legacy depending on the amount of money spent after he was dead. The thought made me feel more ill than I already was.

My fingers played idly with the emerald ring in my pocket. One of the small reminders I had from the good times with Jack. I hadn't stepped foot in a church since my mother died. Yet, here I was, stepping into a church once more due to the awful inevitable fact of death. A death that I was somewhat responsible for...again. I shook the thought from my head and walked through the intimidatingly large doors.

The service would be called beautiful by some, I guess. I don't remember much of it. I was distracted by my solid black suit that was causing me to sweat bullets. The people in the pew in front of me were discussing my red tie and how disrespectful it was, but honestly, it was the only one I owned. I ignored them. Honestly, as the priest spoke, all I could focus on was the casket that held Jack's corpse. It was a gorgeous deep mahogany wood with gold accents; simple and elegant. Not the type of casket I would have expected Jack to pick out for himself. Not black or flashy enough, I thought to myself.

As the priest called everyone up to say their final goodbyes, my heart dropped. Did I want to see Jack like this? Would the image of Jack laying in that casket be forever burned over my memories of him happy and alive? As I watched the few others in the church go up, my feet began to move before I was ready to reconcile with what I was about to see. I had to. I never had a chance to properly say goodbye on that last night.

In death, Jack somehow looked less pale than he had in life. Whoever did his make-up had skipped the eyeliner he frequently wore, but didn't skip the dark eye shadow or his favorite red lipstick. Wrapped around him was that black dress he loved so much; that Gideon hated. Fitting for a funeral with its red sash around the waist and matching red silk underskirt. The black lace around the top looked like feathers against his skin.

Everything felt and looked fake, like a wax figure as opposed to Jack's actual body. My mind raced with every detail of Jack alive and I wondered if seeing him like this was a mistake. This wasn't Jack. I should have followed my gut reaction and left the memories I had alone.

The priest coughed, signaling that I was probably staying a bit too long, but I didn't want to leave. Tears filled my eyes and I squeezed them shut, biting my tongue as I breathed sharply through my nose. Not here. Not in front of Gideon. I wouldn't let him see my pain. He couldn't know that he had won. I would not give him that satisfaction. As I returned to my seat, I caught Gideon staring at me from the corner of my eye. Watching me like a hawk and I could have sworn he was smiling.

Jack was interred in Gideon's family mausoleum. Despite his hatred for his husband, Gideon still gave him a millionaire's funeral and burial. Still treated him like the family that he was supposed to be. Jack's family did not want his body,

I assumed, especially given the manner of his death. So he was buried with the past generations of Bellviews, where Gideon would go when he died as well. So much for 'til death do us part. Anger bubbled and rolled in my stomach at the thought. The interment was almost impossible to stomach since I was the only one besides Gideon who knew the truth. I knew it was all a charade. Gideon had murdered Jack and he was going to get away with it.

As people left the cemetery, Gideon sat down on the stairs of the mausoleum. Crocodile tears ran down his brick of a face, threatening to show the faults and cracks. Bright rays of sunshine beamed down, making his black suit somehow blacker. He stood out like Death itself against the white of the marble stairs.

"Gideon." I said, slowly approaching the "grieving" man. His face was buried in his hands now and his shoulders moved erratically as he sobbed. Everyone had left. Why was he still putting on this charade? "Gideon." I said, louder this time and standing before him. Even sitting down, Gideon was still up to my chest.

"Go away." The words were snarled and punctuated by a deep snort as he spit a ball of phlegm in my direction.

"I know you killed him." My eyes bore holes

through Gideon. The anger spread through my blood. Clenching my fists and teeth, I snarled. "I know you fucking killed him." Gideon looked up at me, his face twisted between grief and confusion.

"Me, kill Jack?" The words were spoken softly. "Judah, what are you even saying?" He actually sounded hurt.

"You. Killed. Jack." I hissed the words, my whole body beginning to tense. The urge to punch him in his fucking face was hard to fight.

"You're out of your mind." Gideon tried to stand and I shoved him down with both my hands. He yelped in surprise, grimacing as his ass met with the hard marble.

"No. Listen to me Gideon Bellview. I know what fucking happened. I know about the abuse, about the beatings. Jack came to me before you killed him. He told me he still planned on leaving you, especially after that stunt with the gun." My eyes locked with Gideon's. He was unmoving. "Jack told me you threatened to kill him if he left. Then he suddenly shows up dead with the same gun you threatened him with?" My shadow covered Gideon and he looked small to me. So much smaller than the towering monster I knew him to be.

"That's exactly what happened." Gideon

looked visibly ill; haunted by whatever images or scenes were playing out in his head. “I could never...”

“Bullshit!” I screamed, grabbing Gideon by his shoulders. “You absolutely could! You beat him! You controlled his whole fucking life!” Gideon tried to push me away but I pushed back, pressing Gideon’s back into the steps. My knee was shoved into Gideon’s stomach, pinning him down with my face inches from his. “You fucking murdered Jack and covered it up as a suicide because he was going to leave you.”

Gideon’s face contorted and I saw my rage reflected in his suddenly bright eyes.

“No one is going to believe you. The poor, pathetic piece of shit who Jack was having an affair with? Please.” Gideon pressed himself into my knee, sneering. “I was at work when it happened, I have witnesses.”

“Liar!” I screamed, wrapping my hands around Gideon’s throat. “You killed him and covered it up!” I wanted to smash his head against those marble stairs more than anything.

Gideon laughed, a wheezing sound that made his neck bulge in my grasp. “The neighbors heard the gunshot. He killed himself, Judah. Accept it.”

"Um, is everything alright, gentleman?" The priest appeared out of nowhere. Gideon and I both looked at him. Letting go of Gideon, I stood and turned to go. "Don't make a scene." I snorted as Gideon's words floated through my mind again. As I walked away, the priest quickly shuffled over to Gideon and helped him up. There was mumbled discussion I couldn't hear as I walked away. Before I left the cemetery, I looked over my shoulder and saw Gideon and the priest still talking. Gideon saw me watching them and smiled. He waved and I retched. So much for the mourning husband bit.

The truth would come out. Gideon Bellview would get what he deserved. I would make sure of it.

XII.

Jack's grave became my new Helena's. Without a job, without a lover, without a purpose, I had nothing better to do than sit on the marble steps and drink. Each day I would arrive when the cemetery gates opened and make the solemn walk to Jack's resting place, pouring some of my whiskey from my flask out next to the mausoleum. I spoke with his ghost frequently. All the conversations I wish we had. All the things we still had yet to do. Planning for a future that would never come. I told him about all the apartments I was looking at and where. I was even looking at adopting a cat, looking particularly at black cats that I knew Jack would have loved. I showed him the ring I never had a chance to give him. The crunch of the gravel on the aptly named Cemetery Drive was becoming an all too familiar sound. It was often the only sound I heard every evening as I left, escorted by the groundskeeper.

Evenings were spent watching Gideon hoping he would slip up, give himself away and somehow confirm my suspicions. His routine seemed unbroken by the untimely death of his husband. Neighbors and coworkers dropped by with gifts and kind words. There were a few I approached, asking them about that night. The shiftiness in their eyes as they answered my questions gave me more than I ever needed to condemn Gideon. Were they paid off? Living in this neighborhood meant they weren't exactly hurting for money. Threatened then? Or was there blackmail involved? Everyone has their dirty little secrets, it would make sense that Gideon would know what leverage he had with everyone else.

During the month we had together, Jack had spoken frequently of his neighbors. He knew of Mrs. Reeves's cocaine addiction, of Mr. Meling fucking Mrs. Roberts. Hell, even the Gordons were swingers who were involved with quite a few of the families on the block. Did Jack relay these stories to Gideon, as he had to me, and now Gideon threatened to tell and shatter their worlds if they dared threaten him? Blackmail wasn't something that seemed to be below Gideon. In fact, it seemed right up his alley.

Talking to the Hendersons was the most revealing. She and her husband lived in a relatively small five bedroom and three bathroom two doors down from Jack and Gideon. She spoke fondly of Jack, who would often come over and help her with the rose garden she dutifully tended. They were one of the few families Jack had not told the secrets of. Either they hid them well, or they were the rarity on the block with none to tell.

"What an awful thing to happen. Poor Gideon." She spoke softly as she poured me a cup of tea, her dark hands contrasting sharply with the plain white kettle. I swallowed large gulps of the tea in a poor attempt to quell my boiling stomach.

"If I remember, I saw you at the funeral, right?" She continued, lips drawn tight as she watched me chug the still steaming drink. "It was a beautiful if...nontraditional service." She refilled it without me even lifting the cup again. I nodded wordlessly.

"Yea. A friend. My name is Judah." I said, staring at her over the rim of my glasses. "Mrs. Henderson, can you tell me about that night?" I sipped my tea while she placed a hand on her chest and looked over at her husband. Mr. Henderson placed a hand on her knee and nodded solemnly.

"Sure. I mean, we were just home watching TV. It sounded like a car backfiring." Mrs. Henderson said. "But louder."

"What were you watching?" I asked, taking another drink.

"Excuse me? I don't...exactly remember.

Some late night show?" She sounded bewildered.

"At 6pm?" I pressed. Mr. Henderson squeezed his wife's hand.

"I don't see the point in this." He interjected.

"I just want some closure, Mr. Henderson." I smiled. "That's all. Jack's death was so sudden and I had just seen him, I just...I just want to put the timeline together." It sounded convincing to me. Not entirely a lie. I wondered if they could smell the alcohol on my breath.

"It may have been a rerun. I'm not exactly too sure. I'm sorry I don't have more information for you." She spoke in a rush. Both of them kept looking at the door which was my cue to leave.

"Thank you for your time. I'm really sorry I dropped by so late, but I was in the area." I spoke as I gathered myself to leave. Mr. And Mrs. Henderson watched with me a cautious regard, their worry reflected in the lines across their faces. "Jack just spoke so highly of you two, I just figured..." I trailed off as I realized that my platitudes were falling short. "Thank you again." I said as I walked through the door, feeling the wind of it quickly closing behind me. Don't let the door hit you on your way out, I grumbled to myself as I walked back to my car.

As I pulled out of the driveway, I could see

them peering through the blinds. Mr. Henderson had a cellphone gripped tightly in his hand. Tea mixed with the acid of my otherwise emptied stomach hit the back of my teeth. Who was he calling? Gideon? My vision faded to white as the anger of betrayal blazed through me. Everyone was in on it. They all knew, but none of them dared challenge Gideon.

The familiar crunch of Cemetery Drive brought me back. In my fury, I had traveled to the only place that brought me solace now – Jack's grave. The street lights cast long shadows from the gates making them appear to be looming. Menacing almost. I turned the car off and sat there, staring at the padlocked gate. Sitting in my passenger seat was the local newspaper. Page 3. "Local Tech Hero Loses Husband in Shocking Suicide". Not only was it wrong, but the same paper had published his obituary before, which talked more about Gideon than it did Jack. The truth was being buried along with Jack. After hearing and seeing the Hendersons, on top of the newspaper article, I knew more than ever that Gideon had murdered Jack. I needed to talk to Jack. He deserved to know that I knew. Sure, I had told him my suspicions, but now they were confirmed.

I picked the lock, a skill I had picked up as a

bored teenager, before opening the creaking gates. The groundskeeper left at 8pm; I only knew that because one night while escorting me out he foolishly told me. Idiot, I thought as I shut the gates behind me.

The way to the mausoleum was long and winding, a concrete path that was only kept due to the money of the graves it led to. Other paths were dirt or barely visible under the weeds and overgrown grass. Large, ominous structures filled with the rotting and skeletal bodies of the rich. I snorted. What a joke. Death doesn't care and we all rot the same. Monuments to money and arrogance, I thought as I passed between them. There were no lights here since the cemetery was not open at night. Memory took me to Jack and the stairs that led up to that white, green and gold structure. Even at night, the patina on the door was clear, but more sickly looking without the warmth of the sun. A wrought iron gate covered the door with another padlock keeping it shut until the next Bellview died.

Until the next Bellview died. The thought brought a smile to my face as I sat on the steps, leaning back against the cool marble. Gideon's family was already gone and Gideon was the only remaining Bellview. He would be the last and that would be it. A truly wonderful thing!

- XII. -

The mausoleum was a simple structure, made of white and gray marble, with the family crest engraved above the door. The crest, a lion standing on two legs with two crossed swords behind, stood in stark contrast with the doves on the stained glass windows. Each dove, one on either side, held an olive branch in its dull yellow beak. Designed by Gideon's great-great-grandmother according to the priest. For a family who came from money and continued to have money, it was one of the plainer mausoleums in this section of the graveyard.

"Jack, if you can hear me, I know he killed you." The words sounded weird and strained against the silence of the night. Most of the time, I didn't speak to Jack out loud. I figured if he was dead and there was really an afterlife, maybe it granted him the ability to read my mind. Plus, I didn't want to get kicked out for being the crazy guy talking to nothing in the middle of a graveyard. The groundskeeper already gave enough weird looks as I drank on these steps day in and day out.

The tears came next. "I'm so sorry I couldn't stop him." I sobbed, taking a long drink the flask I kept on me at all times now. "I'm sorry I wasn't there for you. I'm sorry...I'm sorry you're dead." My whole body shuddered and shook as I sobbed. The first real cry since Jack had died. Sorrow ripped through my body uncontrollably. Every muscle in my body seizing and tensing with each breath and sob. I screamed. I smashed my flask on the stair repeatedly in a fit, hard enough to dent it. I wept. Emotions ripped through me, slipping away only to be replaced by a new one before I could even identify them.

"I'm so fucking sorry. I'm so sorry I'm so sorry I'm so sorry." The saltiness of tears and snot mingled with the whiskey in my mouth. I took another swig, gagging and vomiting as it got caught in my throat. My whole body ached and I felt so defeated. Jack was gone and all I had were the memories, a few of his things, and the ring.

Reaching in my pocket, I pulled out the ring, watching it glimmer in the moonlight. Jack would have loved it. My heart ached at the fact that Jack would never get to wear it. Returning it was never an option. So, I held onto it. Rolling it across my fingers, I took a deep breath. What the fuck was I going to do? I stared at the ring I had never given to Jack. A broken promise...

Jack deserved everything in the God damned world and Gideon took that from him. Ever since the very beginning, Gideon destroyed any chance of a life for Jack. There was only one solution. One thing that would quell this duress and give Gideon what he deserved. Gideon had paid off the whole block or at least dangled blackmail in front of them. No one would say anything. He had the whole world fooled that Jack had killed himself. He didn't deserve the peace and pity everyone was giving him.

I could still feel Gideon's throat in my hands. The feeling of his throat bulging under my palms as he laughed and mocked me. A familiar and hot rage ripped through my gut as I felt the want to smash his head against the very stairs I sat on. Killing Gideon would have felt amazing. It wouldn't bring Jack back, nothing would, but fuck it would have felt incredible.

Then it came to me again. Until the next Bellview died. Gideon would get a fucking bullet between the eyes. If there was a Hell, Gideon Bellview would be going there and I would personally see to it. Gideon didn't deserve to live after what he did to Jack. I clenched my fists tightly and ground my teeth against the nausea rising in my throat. He deserved to die and I was going to make sure of it.

It would be easy too. Gideon had a gun. A husband so distraught in grief over his husband's suicide that he kills himself too. Just like he did to Jack, only this time there would be no one to avenge him. No one who would know or even seek the truth.

Poor Gideon, the words Mrs. Henderson has said earlier brought the bile to behind my teeth. Poor Gideon indeed.

With a renewed sense of purpose, I wished Jack goodnight and left. The security gate over the door felt supernaturally cold under my warm hand. The coldness of Death. I shivered despite the sweat dripping down my back and turned to leave. There were plans to be made.

From under my bed, I slipped out the sleek black case that held my handgun. Jack didn't even know it was there. Something I had bought back in Georgia for "home protection." It hadn't been fired since the day I bought it and brought it to the range to test it, but I figured it would fire all the same now, right? It felt heavier than I remembered in my hands. The sleek black body reflected the light from the lamp on my nightstand, catching the subtle glow of the clock on my nightstand. That red gleam made it seem more sinister as my mind wandered.

I'd shove this gun down Gideon's throat, like I believed he had done to Jack. Everything he ever did to Jack, I would relay it to him as I made him choke. The thought of Gideon's eyes in these moments made me shudder with glee. I wouldn't stop there. He would beg and cry for his life, just like Jack did. Hoping somewhere at the back of his mind and deep in his heart that I would spare him. That maybe he could make it all better with money or, knowing Gideon, threatening me if I did kill him. In reality, I would really make him experience the fear and terror that was a daily occurrence for Jack. Then, I would pull the trigger and bang, no more Gideon Bellview. The thought brought a smile and a chuckle as I shifted the unloaded weapon between my hands and appreciated its heft. No more Gideon, no more Bellviews, a legacy and a story coming to an end, as it deserved.

Revenge. Pure and simple. The need for revenge runs deep in people. A one-way street that supposedly led to families and victims sleeping better. Something that never made sense to me until now. But, the world would be a better place without Gideon. There would never be another victim like Jack, not if I had anything to do with it. Could this be called justice? I wasn't so sure, but did it matter? There was no justice in this story. I grimaced. Jack deserved justice, poetic or not. Revenge doesn't fix anything. It doesn't bring the dead back. Nothing does. Not the murder of one or a thousand evil men. And yet, here I was with a gun in my hand and planning to enact it.

One thing bothered me though. Gideon would be buried with Jack. He would die a mourning husband so stricken by grief that he followed his husband into death. Gideon would die someone worthy of being mourned and being missed. Jack's suicide was something seen as unforgivable and Gideon's would be seen as understandable. The thought didn't sit right with me. There was no justice for Jack in that. Gideon needed his name destroyed, just like he had destroyed Jack's life. That would be justice and not just revenge. Everyone needed to know the real Gideon, the Gideon that Jack and I knew.

A suicide note then, perhaps? Just like in the movies, written with a gun pointed at the back of his head. Maybe then, I could even get Gideon to commit suicide with his own gun and leave no trace of me behind. It seemed as foolproof as Gideon's plan to kill Jack. Gideon deserved this. He deserved it long before he was able to carry it to its brutal end. Jack didn't deserve all the pain and suffering Gideon brought.

Tears ran anew down my face as I thought of Jack and his life. The promise of our lives together had seemed so bright and promising. It seemed almost foolish that we believed we could escape it. Yet, what else did we have other than to try? The alternative was too painful to bear and yet, that was the reality I was left with. Not the apartment across the country. No pets to care for together. No white picket fence or playground with our kids – I didn't even know if Jack wanted to have kids. All of it gone. No Jack. No future. Nothing but loneliness and whatever would come next.

"I miss you. I miss you so much." I sobbed to nothing. To the darkness. To the ghost of Jack. Emotions swelled through me once again as they had in the cemetery. A poor attempt to fill the emptiness that had grown inside of me. An emptiness that felt like it was growing out of control and threatening to swallow me alive. Grief turned to loneliness turned to pain. Nothing fit and felt right. It all felt wrong, every single emotion trying and failing. There was another option I hadn't considered, but that lurked dark in the back of my mind. Joining Jack and seeing whatever came next. I squeezed my eyes shut, feeling the tears burning. No, now was not the time to lose myself to grief, I told myself. Not yet. Gideon needed to be sent to Hell first and if that damned me with him, I would face those consequences later.

XIII.

As I pulled up to the mansion, the clock on my dashboard read 9:42pm. Enough time to seem like I was just someone arriving late to a party or something and wouldn't be strange if I left late too. I parked on the other block, making sure to park in an alley next to a house that still had their lights on. My many trips through the neighborhood helped me know all the weird alleys and side streets. Hopefully no one would think anything about it. The neighbors on the street Gideon lived on knew my vehicle by now. I would wait until later and hope that parking here and being here for awhile would be enough to give me an alibi if I needed it. Plus, no one would be awake still by the time I made my way to the mansion.

Waiting to leave the car, my mind reeled. Was this plan too complicated? Too simple? Too stupid? What if someone saw me just sitting in my car? No matter what I did I could not calm my shaking hands or anxious heart. Despite just sitting and waiting, I felt like I had run a mile. I was panting and wheezing, struggling to try and breathe. What was I doing here?

Was I really plotting to murder someone? And yet, when the time came, I slipped out of my car and made my way to Gideon's mansion. It was too late to change my mind now.

Every single light was on as I walked quickly to the mansion. There were lights on in rooms that probably had not seen another human in them besides a maid in years. Never mind that it was 2am on a Wednesday and everyone in this part of the neighborhood was asleep or out on a cocaine bender. At least, that is what I assumed rich business tyrants did on a Wednesday night. Tonight, Gideon was waiting for me, though I could not say for sure there was no cocaine involved in that decision.

The lights made the house glow eerily and making the windows look like the reflective eyes of a predator. So many eyes supernaturally bright in the night. All of them focused on me with a knowing gaze. Even the red door seemed to be darker than usual, almost black, under the porch light. My mind flashed to Jack sprawled across my bed, not asleep, but dead. The mansion seemed to breathe in anticipation of my arrival, expanding and contracting with each step I took towards it. A true house of horrors. I drained my flask in order to calm my nerves.

I didn't even bother to try and sneak into the house. The doorknob tuned easily as the heavy oak door swung silently on its hinges, temporarily blinding me with the light held within. Gideon had left the front door unlocked. He definitely was expecting me, but how? Why? No one in the world knew my plan, besides Jack. How does that old saying go? Dead men tell no tales? So, how did Gideon know to wait for me? Unless, he saw me outside on those nights watching him. Even then, why was he ready tonight?

"Yes, yes. Come right on in, Judah. Make yourself at home!" Gideon's singsong voice echoed from the kitchen. My fingers grazed the cool metal of the handle of the gun in my hand. The only other noise was Gideon rustling around in the kitchen with the faint clanking of glass giving him away. A rather lighthearted sound. As Gideon rounded the corner, a cocktail in each hand, I raised the gun.

The living room of the mansion was surprisingly sparse. A leather couch with two matching recliners and a coffee table. An open design that had a little breakfast nook leading to the kitchen and from what I could see, a dining room with an over-sized dining table. The walls were filled with various rewards given to Gideon and his companies. The space felt large and empty, barely lived in. A show of wealth and power as opposed to a home.

"I know why you are here. You can stop making a show of it. Sit. Sit." The way he talked made the hairs on my neck and arms stand on end. Not a care in the world. He didn't care about the gun pointed at him. He didn't care that Jack was dead. He didn't care it was his fault. Carefree. When I did not move, he gestured to one of the leather armchairs in the expansive entryway.

"Sit." That cold and commanding voice. It shot through my heart. The same way he talked to Jack. Had talked to Jack. Cold. Indifferent. More like talking to an annoyance than your husband. The person you're supposed to love. I kept my gun pointed at him, circling to stand across the room from him. Keeping the door at my back in case I needed to make a quick getaway.

"He's dead because of you." The words slid past my lips. Burning. The words were hard to say and yet here, they came out so effortlessly despite that pain or maybe, because of that pain. Gideon had to know what he did. Had to know he wasn't going to get away with murder.

"No. He's dead because he killed himself. I wasn't the one who decided to well, you know." Gideon placed the drinks on the coffee table as he spoke. He then placed his fingers to his head to mime a gun and then made a cartoonish gun firing noise. Gideon's massive form lowered to sit on the couch, resting his arms on the back of it. Despite his size, he didn't even sink into the soft leather. My blood boiled, my anxiety being replaced with anger. Jack was barely cold in his grave and he was already making jokes about his death? Air hissed passed my teeth. He still talked so plainly about the events, as if there were years between them as opposed to just days. How could he have moved on already? Was there no remorse or guilt in this man? Did he even truly feel emotion? My finger tensed on the trigger, threatening to shoot him dead now. Not yet, he had to admit what he had done first.

"You're a liar! It's all your fault!" I was screaming. The gun shook wildly in my hands. "He had nothing! You made sure of that!" Every fiber of my body was on fire. All the rage. The sorrow. The hurt. "I can prove it was you!" Spit flew from my lips as I yelled like a rabid animal.

"Oh can you now?" Gideon raised a bushy eyebrow.

"I waited for him. I never saw him. You killed him and then when you realized you couldn't move and hide a body, you staged it like a suicide." My throat was hoarse and it hurt to talk, but I had to make Gideon admit it.

"Judah." Like an annoyed parent trying to sooth a child during a temper tantrum. Did he even see the gun in my hands? "He ran away. The police brought him back in the middle of the night. Apparently he was staying with the Hendersons."

"Bullshit! I spoke with them. I saw them call you when I left."

"They called me because they were worried a drunk was going to come banging on my door." Gideon laughed, slapping his knee. "If only they knew how right they were! The same night even!" He laughed harder.

"And what about the threats? How did you say it? If Jack wanted to leave he would 'leave in a body bag'?" I stepped forward which caused Gideon to shift his weight, his icy eyes now focused on the gun.

"He could have stayed." Gideon said, eyes locking onto mine. There was not a hint of remorse. No humanity hidden in those depths. Just a cunning. A dare. He took a sip of the drink, gesturing again towards mine.

"With you? A monster?" The words bubbled out of my mouth and my throat on fire. Instinctively I reached for my flask, but it was empty. That glass on the table looked so tempting and I swallowed hard. "You're a fucking monster, Gideon."

"We're not so different. You and I. Only I was successful while your business failed. Isn't that right?" Gideon spoke coldly, but the words cut like a knife.

"We're nothing alike. I loved Jack. You used him." I snarled, feeling my lip curl back to expose my teeth. There were tears streaming down my face that I couldn't control.

"Really? You showered Jack with gifts, placing yourself in a significant amount of debt to buy Jack's love." Gideon grinned, puffing his chest out in perceived victory.

"I gave him everything he wanted. As he deserved. I didn't give him gifts to say 'sorry for abusing you'." Gideon raised his hands and I could see the panic starting to set in as I refused to drop the gun. I kept my finger on the trigger and I could see him nervously glancing at it.

"You don't know anything about me." I spat. I blinked the tears from my eyes to keep my vision from blurring. The last thing I wanted was for Gideon to see me lose complete control.

"Oh, I know much more than you think, Judah Moretti. What's the real reason you never moved home? Did you tell Jack about Georgia?" Gideon took a drink, his eyes never leaving me. The corners of his lips started to twitch upwards, sensing another way to get to me.

"Of course." My hands had began to shake, and I lowered the gun. It suddenly felt like dead weight in my hands. Where was Gideon going with this?

"Did you *really* tell him? Does he know about your business partner? Oh what was his name..." Gideon snapped his fingers as he thought. "Oh yes," a sneer crept across that flat sculpted face. "Ethan. That *was* his name." My arms fell as Gideon said that name, the gun thumping dully on my thigh. Ethan's name struck me in the heart – a name I hadn't heard in years. A name I wish I could forget but was always there at the back of my mind. "I wouldn't be your first kill, would I?"

"Shut up," I whispered.

"Poor Ethan. You were drunk and dumb. Wrapped your car around a tree and made it out without a scratch. But poor, poor Ethan. Ejected from the car and -" Gideon ended his sentence by clapping his heads together. I grimaced in disgust.

"Shut up."

Gideon continued. "Your business failed soon

after. Then your mother died. Tragedy just follows you, doesn't it, Judah?" Gideon's sneer turned into a grin, his all too white teeth gleamed in the bright light of the living room.

"Just. Shut. Up." I growled the words through clenched teeth. The metal of the gun bit into my hand as I clutched the grip tightly. My eyes squeezed shut in an effort to strangle the tears.

"Ethan. Your mother. Jack. Who's next?" A slight pause. "I guess it's me, huh?" Gideon laughed. A deep, resonating sound. So sure of himself. He was so fucking sure of himself. "No wonder that pathetic little whore-"

"Fuck you." If you've never fired a gun, you're not ready for the sound. The outdoor range didn't prepare me for the sudden concussive burst that seems to shatter the world for a second. No ear protection to cut it down in the slightest. One second and it's done. That's all it takes. The bullet travels through the air and hits something eventually. The ground. A beer bottle. A target. Gideon fucking Bellview.

"You don't get to insult Jack like that. Not anymore." Before I realized what was happening, I fired a second round into Gideon as he clutched at his chest. His eyes wide with fear. I realized then that he didn't think I would do it. He didn't think I had the guts to shoot him. All movement stopped with that second shot as my ears rang and my vision swam.

Death isn't like it is in the movies. Everyone knows that. I don't think anyone is really prepared for how degrading it is. I stood there, staring at Gideon slowly bleeding out on the couch. Blood pooled under his feet and on the cushions, dripping down the leather. I don't know how long I stood there, consumed by the ringing that drowned out everything but my own blood rushing through my body. My legs felt weak underneath me as I swayed with the room spinning around me.

As Gideon lay there, dead or dying on his several-thousand-dollar couch, my legs took me around the house. Searching. I didn't know what I was looking for until I found it. The bathroom. The place where Jack had lay, bleeding on the floor. It looked pristine. Shining. Beautiful. The floor was various shades of gray, meant to imitate wood as opposed to tile. On the far wall under the window was a massive clawfoot bath tub and two stand alone sinks. I could imagine which one was Jack's as it had already been cleared of all of his personal effects. The toilet was in a separate corner with its own door along with a standing shower. Then my eyes saw the bullet hole in the wall. Small and dark against the wall behind the bath tub. No trace of the horrific loss of life that had happened within its confines.

The tile was cool. That was the only thing I thought as I laid on that floor with my knees pulled to my chest. Time meant nothing on that floor. I cried. I screamed. I beat the floor and wailed until my hands were raw and red. Every emotion that I had channeled into those bullets to murder Gideon Bellview were now bubbling back up and spilling out. And why the fuck did I keep saying his name!? Hell, there were parts of me that I still don't think quite fully comprehended that I had just killed him. He is dead because of me. The thought bounced around my head much like the ringing of the gun shots.

Everything was on fire. The pain and the agony. The absolutely desperate feeling of loneliness and loss. Every negative emotion flooding through all at once. I needed it to end. Jack could make it end. I just had to go to Jack. We could be together and then it would never hurt. It would never ever hurt like this again...that emptiness filled and swallowed me. Did Gideon get what he deserved? Will I get what I deserve?

The cold metal and acrid taste of gunpowder pulled me back to reality. The click of me cocking the gun kicked me in the gut. I slowly pulled the gun from my mouth, knocking my teeth against the barrel. Slowly, I got up and left. I walked right past Gideon's corpse, right out the front door. I left it swinging wide and proud. Gideon's dead body in full view of the whole fucking world. Finally getting what he deserved way too late. The damage had been done.

I thought killing Gideon would make everything go away. That it would make me feel better that in some way so that Jack's death wasn't in vain. I thought it would make the pain go away. That maybe closing that chapter on Jack's life would make it end for me too. I thought of so many different excuses and ideas to justify my actions. Regardless of what I came to, it all pointed to the same conclusion: the world was better without Gideon Bellview. Maybe Jack would be happy about that. Or maybe he would be disappointed in me.

And yet, the pain was still there. Jack was still gone. And I had to figure out what to do with my life now. Killing Gideon brought no sudden revelation or clarity. There was no direction to be gleamed from this act of violence and I was still as lost as I was before. Still as hollow as I had felt on that bathroom floor with a loaded gun, cocked and ready to fire, pressed to the back of my throat.

No one but me knew what truly had

happened to Jack. Gideon would not face the justice he deserved. He would die a victim of senseless violence, gunned down in his own home by a criminal. How long did I have? My freedom was surely fleeting. What did anyone do when they knew their time was limited? I had no bucket list and doubted I would have time to complete one anyway.

The padlock of the mausoleum rattled against the iron gate it kept shut. The same type used on the gates to the cemetery. Everything felt cold under my hands. The groundskeeper would be here soon. And then, what next? Surely the police would come looking for me. Two shots fired. Potentially armed suspect on the run. Two glasses indicating the victim knew the killer. Surely some hair and fiber in the bathroom if they knew to look there.

Before me the mausoleum stood open and dark. It smelled of dust and faintly of decay. You would think something full of corpses would smell worse, I thought. From the inside, I could see that the stained glass windows let in no light due to the years of dirt and grime that had built up. The dead do not peer out like the living peer in.

The chirping of the birds came followed shortly by the first rays of morning sun. Mourning doves, I thought and I couldn't help but smile softly at the irony of it all. Light broke through the grime, creating long and foreboding shadows that threatened to hide more than just the caskets inside the crypt.

Against the back wall lay Jack's casket. A deep mahogany wood that had a sheen on it that had been long lost on the others. A few of the caskets were starting to deteriorate; long past trying to stand up to the test of time. The shadows made it impossible to see if they had begun to spill their contents as well. I sighed softly feeling the familiar sting of tears well up in my eyes.

My hands were shaking as I placed that emerald ring on top of Jack's casket. The wood felt warm underneath my hands despite the coolness inside the crypt. Both my hands pressed hard – as if I was trying to resurrect him. I wasn't a saint nor was I Jesus. Jack was gone. Forever. Tears slid down my cheeks and I did nothing to wipe them away or stop them as they fell. Time passed and I just stared at the emerald ring on that mahogany wood. It was beautiful.

Reluctantly I lifted my hands and turned to leave. As I looked back, the ring seemed to be alight with an internal fire in the morning sun.

"We tried." I whispered to no one before shutting the door of the mausoleum.

About The Author

Lucian Clark was born and raised in South New Jersey. Their works have been featured across numerous platforms such as *The Advocate* and in anthologies like *Werewolves Versus* and *Postcards From The Void*. They've also been featured on several podcasts to talk about horror, activism, and their writing. With a passion for all things spooky, horrific, and queer, Lucian can often be found on social media talking about werewolves, rats, and My Chemical Romance.

When not actively writing or reading, Lucian is also the curator of the queer horror website, *GenderTerror*, which features original art, stories, interview and more. They can also be found playing video games or with their pets (currently some rats and a cat). They are active in local and national social activism with a focus on LGBTQ+ rights and reproductive justice.

Made in the USA
Middletown, DE
10 November 2022

14569320R00097